# JL WILLIAMS

**author**HOUSE®

*AuthorHouse™*
*1663 Liberty Drive*
*Bloomington, IN 47403*
*www.authorhouse.com*
*Phone: 833-262-8899*

*Published by AuthorHouse  12/02/2021*

*ISBN: 978-1-6655-4622-5 (sc)*
*ISBN: 978-1-6655-4625-6 (e)*

*Library of Congress Control Number: 2021924542*

*Print information available on the last page.*

# Contents

# Dedication

*I* am deeply moved by the support of family and friends. Mostly and especially for this book, I am grateful for the Williams Family, who helped with the editing of Faith Now. At the time it was titled American Zombie. They never waiver in love and support. Many Thanks!

# Chapter 1

## *Just the Beginning*

Tom and Jasmine watched through their condominium window above the city lights and stared at the street below. Normally, there was a low roar of sounds that could be heard through their window. It consisted of people talking, car horns blowing, sirens passing, and doors slamming. But now it was deathly quiet. The silence was the hollowing effects of an earthquake that ran up the Andreas fault line and affected all of California.

It was not only California that was feeling the aftermath from this type of disaster. There were earthquakes, torrential weather of all varieties, and volcanic eruptions simultaneously occurring worldwide. There were miscellaneous disasters as well. Nuclear plants had been compromised, which led to evacuations from the towns that were exposed to radiation or harmed by the outspreading of contaminated water. A spiritual dark cloud was forming, not just in Los Angeles but in different parts of the world.

The news broadcasts conventionally consisted of international news regarding the outbreak of civil wars, government overthrows, and the need for United Nations intervention for peace and other disarmament treaties, as well as whatever was happening in the news locally. But tonight, it was different. It was all about the latest news that was hot off the wire.

The report of civil wars for the moment had been quieted, as people joined together during a time of crisis. People were too busy mourning for the dead from the catastrophic events that were occurring all over the world. Everyone now hungered for a sense of normality that would not come. In masses, people fled to churches, mosques, synagogues, and the like for comfort. Unfortunately, there was also mass hysteria in affect. All over the world, people were wailing and crying in their houses and streets, but not on Tom and Jasmine's street; it was disturbingly quiet.

Jasmine picked up the phone after it rang only once. From the caller ID, she could see it was her dear friend Penny. "Hello," she said. "I know. It's horrible. Yes, you can, but be careful. I'll see you shortly. Love you too." She hung up the phone and looked at her husband, Tom. He gave her a look of concern. "She will be all right. After all, how bad can it be? It's relatively quiet right now," Jasmine said. She patted the side of her large canine friend. She again stared down at the street beneath her.

Penny tried not to look in her rearview mirror as she headed home. She had the radio on and heard reports of looting and vandalism in different cities, especially in Los Angeles. She didn't want to imagine that she was being followed. "I don't understand how everyone can go so wild when calamity strikes," she exclaimed through her Bluetooth mic that dangled from her ear.

Kelso had been trying to get her to agree to put a speakerphone in her car, but she'd insisted it was too much trouble for her dusty blue 1982 Chevelle Malibu Classic Wagon. In truth, she took extremely good care of her somewhat beat-up Chevelle. But Penny refused to upgrade her stereo or add a GPS device. She wanted to keep everything the same when it came to "True Blue," her name for the car.

"I can tell you're driving too fast. Don't get freaked out. You have to remember that this, too, shall pass. Penny?" He paused to listen for her voice. "Are you listening to me? "How far are you from home?" Kelso asked with reservation. He was afraid she was headed down Interstate 85, where there were major delays.

"Not far. I got off of work early. I picked up a couple of things that should help us out in the long run," she said.

A dog growled in the seat behind her.

"What? Was that growling?" asked Kelso. The dog in the back seat barked as if to affirm his identity. "Did you pick up a stray dog? Is it temporary? How freaked out are you? What do you mean by 'the long run'? It may take some time, but everything will settle down. We will get through this. This will not be permanent for any of us," Kelso said.

Penny could hear the concern in Kelso's voice, which only added to her anxiety. He was always the calm one in their relationship. But she considered herself the most logical, except when she became emotional; then all bets were off. Penny now looked into her rearview mirror and spotted a beat-up red Mustang gaining on her. She was not about to pull over, but she was definitely going to try to give them room to pass.

"I will explain about Fido when I get there. I just think. for the time, being we might be safer if we have a dog. It was a gift," Penny said. She was feeling uncomfortable and wanted to change the subject.

"I have never understood, nor will I understand, the mob mentality. It scares me. Did you pick up everything I told you to pick up?" Penny asked anxiously. She again eyed the car behind her, which was closely tailing True Blue. She wished it had already passed. Kelso's words, *This, too, shall pass,* came to mind. She smiled to herself as if it were a confirmation to stay calm and not overreact. Certain things Kelso said, whether they were from the Bible or elsewhere, seemed to resonate with her when she needed his words the most.

The Mustang whizzed by her passenger-side window. She pretended not to notice as the driver laid on the horn, and voices from the Mustang shouted something in her direction. Normally, she would have at least given them the finger, but they were the least of her worries for today.

Kelso heard the horn but said nothing. He waited for Penny to honk back, but she did not. "Not everything, but I was planning on running out later," answered Kelso, "that is, unless you want me at home." He was hoping he would not have to run out later for extra supplies. He was already engrossed with the news and planned on staying that way. Kelso heard a car fly by the house with intermediate honks and shouts. He visualized some kids driving and partying like it was the end of days. They did not get very much traffic on their road and hoped it would stay quiet.

"We'll just have to make due. We have our backup generator, enough water for a couple of months, and lots of dry and canned foods, including powdered milk, just in case we need to make our own bread." She sounded pleased, as if she had thought of everything. Kelso was not sure of the connection between powdered milk and the preferred ingredients that went into a loaf a bread, but he was pretty sure they did not necessarily need powdered milk to make a loaf of bread. But he said nothing.

Penny saw their white fence along the road. "I'm turning into our driveway now. Did you want to help me unload the car?" It was rhetorical.

Penny watched as the porch light turned on and the front door opened to their partial brick, combination Tudor / ranch-style home. Kelso came out of the house dressed in his work attire of Bahama shorts and a plain navy shirt. His straight brown hair caught the wind, and he wiped it from his forehead. Penny could see his thin smile. She could hardly wait to compare stories with her husband. She quickly got out of the car.

As Kelso approached the car, Penny threw her arms around his neck and hugged him. She just held him firmly, her head resting against his shoulder. The dog in the back seat started barking and panting as she prolonged their hug. Kelso now knew she was officially freaked out.

Kelso did not worry too much about Penny's anxiety. But he remembered a time when Penny had almost lost it mentally. It was after they had graduated from college and before he started graduate school. Kelso knew her well back then. They were college sweethearts and spent much of their time together. During their courtship, he never once saw her become unglued.

It was when she started her job interview process that she started to question everything. It was then that Kelso started to see Penny unravel bit by bit. She became unsure of everything. It was if she had lost her footing.

What had the last four years been for? Were her scholastics achievements enough to get a decent job? Would it be enough to go forward and make something of herself? And to what end? Then there was the ultimate question, unbeknown to Kelso, which would cause her heart to beat faster every time she thought about it. How would her quintessential life change, especially without Kelso? At heart, Penny was a simple girl who was not sure how to deal with change.

Kelso knew she was different than the other girls he had dated. She may have been the most attractive woman he'd ever dated, but it was in a well-rounded way. She definitely was the tallest, at five foot eleven, but it was her calm and quiet spirit of contentment that really made her attractive to him.

Penny never talked about commitment or the future. She just seemed to appreciate the time she had with him. He appreciated and loved that about her. He may have even let himself take her sentiments for granted because she was so easygoing. He also noted that she looked at things in a microscopic way, focusing on the smaller parts of a situation. She did not always see the forest from the trees, which was the opposite of how he looked at everything. Details were lost for some people, but not for his Penny.

During college, Kelso noticed how quiet Penny would become at times and zone out, but it was nothing compared to how she was when she was interviewing for her next big venture, after they'd graduated. It was almost impossible to get her attention. She was always somewhere else. Eventually, the pressure of moving, parting ways with Kelso, and obtaining a new job got to her.

Penny admitted herself for psychiatric evaluation after she started the interviewing process for jobs out of state in Wyoming. Kelso, to this day, was not sure why she had admitted herself but thought he could see God's hand in it. There had been nothing definitive about their relationship up until that point. But Kelso did not understand why there needed to be more. He had at least another two years of school before he would be pursuing anything long term, which included a job, house, car, or wife.

Penny had come up with a plan for herself that would take her away from California where Kelso would be attending school. She would find a job that would pay well for at least a year. She would stay with her parents for that year, which would give her residency so she could pay under $15,000 per year to attend her school of choice, University of Wyoming. It was much less than what Kelso would pay for his graduate program at UCLA. At the time, it made her smile, as she was secretly mad at Kelso.

She would continue her education like Kelso but somewhere new. Within the year she would apply for admission to law school. Hopefully, if all went right, she could obtain her jurist doctorate from the University of Wyoming in Laramie. Laramie was located only two and half hours from her parents' house in Casper. In three to four years after graduating college she would start an exciting new vocation as a law clerk, perhaps for her father's practice and eventually have her own practice. She was pleased with her perfect plan—as perfect as her plan could be without Kelso.

After all, the University of Wyoming seemed like the best choice. It had a small enrollment of seventy-one, but she thought she would most likely be excepted. It was not one of the leading law schools. In fact, it was ranked by *U.S. News & World Report* 129th of the top law schools in the nation. But as far as learning to prepare briefs and legal contracts it was rated higher, number 14. Since she wasn't sure what type of law she wanted to specialize in, she especially appreciated the rank of fourteen for legal writing, since it was applicable to any type of law she would choose—intellectual property, real estate, telecom, tax, or even judicial. But her plan would have to wait.

She admitted herself for evaluation for twenty-four hours and then forty-eight hours. Kelso tried to convince Penny that it wasn't necessary, but she insisted. Penny's heart would race when she thought about changing her life in such bold degrees as moving back home and starting a new career while the love of her life would stay in sunny California and continue his education. After being evaluated, she was diagnosed with slight depression and an anxiety disorder. The doctor gave her a prescription antidepressant, which acted as a dopamine and a norepinephrine reuptake inhibitor and so helped with both her anxiety and her depression.

Kelso immediately knew after Penny had spent those

few days over the weekend away from him that Penny would be the one with whom he would spend the rest of his life. It was not because he was head over heels in love with her. Although he loved her, it was not only for this reason he decided on the marriage proposal. He was not in the habit of analyzing his emotions as to how much he loved Penny, but it was during that break that he knew he could not live without her. It was for this reason alone.

After that, Kelso only waited a week to ask Penny to marry him. He would have waited only a couple of days except that he wanted to first ask her parents for their blessing for her hand in marriage. It was an old-fashioned touch but he would want to the option to give his blessing if they were to have a daughter.

He originally never intended on moving to Wyoming but told her, if she had her heart set on that location, he would pick up and go, though for the most part he'd been bred a southern California guy. Penny, from that point on, saw Kelso and life in a different way all together. She didn't know why things had changed with Kelso, but she knew she was blessed with more than she deserved.

Penny told herself she would not become unraveled again. She would make healthy changes to her life. She would try not to retreat into herself. And now, with the world in such disorder, she was proud of herself for staying so focused. She remembered that her counselor said the fact that she faded out sometimes was the way she processed things, and it was fine. But Kelso insisted it was ADHD, an attention disorder. Penny had been fine for years now, as she ate higher protein foods and exercised with the energy of a puppy. Kelso knew, if she did have

ADHD as he had thought, that diet and exercise would be prescribed as the natural way to overcome it.

Penny also gave up the antidepressant after she married Kelso, as she no longer had anxiety attacks or depression. She became much more regimented in her daily routine and started to reach out more to her community and also different environmental causes. She saw herself as mostly perfect, although she did not think of herself as less humble than anyone else. She was a hard-core perfectionist who lacked humility.

Kelso looked down at her and smiled. "It will be OK. Let's get going and unload the car," he said.

Penny looked up at him and gently pushed him away. Still excited, she began reciting the list of items she had picked up from memory and enumerated the importance of such items. Kelso knew that they still couldn't be prepared for what was in store for the both of them.

Kelso interrupted Penny just as she was going over some of the camping gear she thought would come in handy that they did not already possess. "So who is this big fellow? Kelso asked as he peered through the slobbered window. "Does he have everything he needs? Did you remember dog food for Fido?"

Penny stiffened and looked at the dog as if she had forgotten about him. She shook her head no. "Actually, I might have some dog food in the back seat. I'm not sure what Jasmine packed for him. It was a last-minute decision to take him home. He's one of her foster dogs. But he seems to be a good dog, right? she asked. "I'm sorry for the surprise, but I think it's for the best. I have been listening to some weird reports of groups of people breaking into houses and taking advantage of the situation," Penny said. She had her car door open and was reaching behind the seat to pet the dog's head. Fido was now trying to get into the front seat of the car.

Kelso looked at Penny and then looked at the dog. "I just wish we could have discussed it," Kelso said as he thought of a thousand reasons a dog was not a good idea. "I still have those items on our list that I need to pick up at the store. I'll just add dog food. I'll get going. If I run out now and get some food for our new friend, instead of later, there should be fewer people. I won't be long. It'll only get worse if I wait." Kelso took his phone but of his pocket and walked toward the car.

Penny leaned into the car and pulled out the dog's leash from inside a small bag. Fido again tried to climb into the front seat. It was then Penny noticed the small bag of food next to the dog's blanket in his carrier. "It can wait; Jasmine packed a small bag of food for Kelso in his carrier. It was next to his blanket," Penny said regretfully, as she had purposely neglected to mention the dog's real name.

Kelso turned back around. "This keeps getting better and better. This is Jasmine's new foster dog, and she named him after me? I thought the foster dog parent, if that is what they are called, weren't supposed to rename the pets." Kelso, for the first time, was about to lose his composure.

"Jasmine, before she gave him to me, explained that she and Tom did not name him. Apparently, that was already the dog's name when they accepted him as a foster pet. She was just hoping she could find him a home before you knew. Jasmine and Tom never intended on giving him to us as a pet. You get it. We're not the ideal couple for a dog, although we do have a yard," Penny said softly.

Kelso then returned to where Penny was standing. "Penny", he said while leaning into her with crossed arms, his eyes never leaving his so-called 'new best friend', that food won't last over the weekend. Should I run out and get more just in case the grocery store gets out of control?" He paused. "Kelso?" asked Kelso.

They both laughed as they stared at the other. Kelso, an oversize mixed breed, was now back in the back seat, as Kelso came close to the car window. It was the first time Penny felt herself relax. Penny handed Kelso the leash, which he handed back to her. Kelso opened the back door of the wagon, grabbed the dog by the collar, and led the dog into their gated front yard. Kelso released the dog by the collar. The part Doberman and, perhaps, collie mix happily trotted into the front yard.

"I can run out later; you don't have to go. We need to figure out our alternatives for different scenarios. We just need to talk. I'm having a tough time wrapping my mind around everything that's happened. It's as if the Mayan-Aztec prophecies are taking hold but just a little later than predicted," she said sheepishly.

"Don't forget about the Incas," Kelso said, jesting. "I don't know what to think about any of this— the earthquakes, the looting, and the crazy officials. They're telling us we can't leave the state. All those poor people with travel plans. But I know it's not the end of civilization," he added.

"Do you think the comet in the North Pacific caused

some of the earth plates to collide? Also, we're only forty miles out from the city. So, what if we are in the hills? We could still be in trouble if times get desperate. Like in the show *Walking Dead*, people could be rioting and looking for places to invade, not that there will be zombies. That's stupid," Penny said as her heart started to race.

His eyebrow raised. "Calm down, woman," Kelso said with a sneer and a smile. He was just as concerned and had twice as many questions but sticking to the facts was a better plan than borrowing from Penny's imagination. "I can wait to go back out after we have gathered more information. There should be some application for our smartphone that we can download that will give us more information as to what's going on with our little town and what roadways are safe to travel."

Penny had a weird smile on her face that displeased Kelso. "Tom told me of an application like that. I'll text Jasmine for the name. I believe it cycles off other drivers with the same application. It competes with the Google and Apple map products, but it doesn't only work off satellite images in the same way, so it may or may not be as accurate. Jasmine said I didn't need it and to just use what I have. But then she did something silly." Penny was quiet for a moment.

The dog whimpered for attention. "Well?", asked Kelso.

The dirt kicked around under her shoes. "Jasmine wanted me to take Tom's smartphone temporarily, but I refused. They tried to sell me on it. She said she felt like I was supposed to have it. Apparently, he had some sort of 'tricked out' smartphone that Jasmine thought would help me. It had some strange features I mean really strange, like seven to the thousandth percent strange."

Kelso looked at his wife's big eyes and wondered what was behind them. "You mean '007' James Bond stuff? It had something like maybe a flashlight?" asked Kelso. "I'm going to have to give you a tour of your phone sometime."

She shook her head and rolled her eyes. "No, it was different than that. It was over my head, but not everything. I swear his phone may have had a Taser attachment. But I didn't want to take Tom's phone even if he had another one. I ended up taking the dog instead. I get the practicality of a dog. Do you know that dogs not only keep you safe but can even predict earthquakes?" As Penny said this, she realized that the information about the GPS application could still be helpful. She texted Jasmine to ask for the name and the details of the application.

"I'm tied into some local media feeds and tweets. I set up a news filter that appears as a banner heading on my smartphone with pertinent information for our area. I will configure your phone, too. It may not be 'tricked out,' but it should help," said Kelso.

"That's fine. Thank you in advance," Penny said and half smiled. She felt foolish knowing as little as she did about technology.

Penny thought of another last-minute item she'd acquired and wasn't sure how to introduce it without once again making a fool of herself. "Speaking of safe and being safe, I know another item that should help. Promise you won't be mad, but Jason gave me one of his guns for protection. He said we could have it." She went to the other side of the car, opened the passenger side door, and pulled a Glock 42 pistol from the glove compartment.

Kelso had always wanted a gun but had shelled that desire when he'd started dating Penny, who was predominately an antigun pacifist. Penny handed the gun to Kelso. This time Kelso didn't hand anything back like he had with the dog's leash.

Kelso held the gun in his, hands looking at it before he switched it to a gun's natural position in his right hand. It weighed a couple ounces less than a pound. It was slim-line perfection; he touched the three-inch barrel with his left hand. He then lifted the gun in front of him as if he was going to shoot it, unlatched the safety, and then latched it again. He checked the magazine, which held six rounds of ammunition.

"I'll teach you how to shoot this gun tomorrow. If you don't have any more hidden surprises, let's go inside." Kelso put his arm around Penny and grabbed one of the bags Penny had set out for him to take inside. He slipped the gun into the bag. They slowly walked inside, leaving the other Kelso to get acquainted with the new surroundings.

As they walked in the house, the answering machine screened a call from Penny's parents. "Anyway, that's our story so far. Well, Penny Money," said her father, using a nickname that had stuck with her from her childhood. "We just wanted to say we love you, and we are all right. We won't be here, but we will call you from your sister's house in the country. Please be careful. Bye."

"Pick up! Kelso, pick up, quickly! Hand me the phone," exclaimed Penny.

Kelso handed Penny the phone. She immediately dialed back her parents. "Damn it, I don't know why they aren't picking up. Kelso, they're not picking up. Why didn't they call my cell phone?"

"They still don't have a cell phone, so they had to use their landline, rather house phone, to call you, and they just left. They will call you when they get there. Don't worry; they'll stay safe," said Kelso.

"I know they still don't have a cell phone and they called from their house, dumbass. Is it a problem that they still don't have a cell phone? How do you know they'll be safe?" spouted Penny. Penny was not unabashed. Kelso could not believe the words that were flowing from his lovely wife's lips. The last time she'd called someone a dumbass was in high school, and it had felt the same way, awkward.

It was classic. Kelso raised his eyebrow. No words were needed. *Heck yes, it's a problem that they do not have a cell phone.*

The call came in again from her parents. Penny picked it up on the half ring. "Hello? Hi, Mom," she said.

"Oh, good, dear, you're there. Dad wants to tell you something. I'm handing the phone to him," said Penny's mother.

"Dad?" Penny said as she wiped her eyes.

The phone was pressed firmly in her father's hand. "Yes, honey. I can't talk long. They say the roads may get crowded. But don't worry about us. We have it all figured out." His voice cracked as he spoke. "I have a cell phone that the Simpsons gave us, from the lot over. I have a cell phone, but I'm not sure what the phone number is."

He gave a half laugh, feeling a little foolish. I am calling you with it, so, if you could tell me what setting to look under, I could tell you what the number is. Or you could put Kelso on."

"Paul, we have to go, or they'll leave without us," said Mom gently as she put her hand on her husband's forearm. Penny could see it all in her mind. Her parents were unsure of what was next on their horizon; but as long as they were together, they could weather anything. But then again, what choice did they have? She thought to herself.

"Just hold on. They won't leave without us. They need us to navigate. It's Nancy's house, remember. Our daughter has to have our phone number, or what use is this darn thing? Penny, how do I get this number off of this thing so you can have it?" asked Penny's dad.

"It's OK, Dad," Penny said as she turned and winked at Kelso. "The phone number that you called from registers on my phone. Who are you traveling with, Dad?"

"So you do have it? Well I'll be. You have this number?" asked Penny's father.

"Yes, Dad. It's 555-354-2758. I also have Nancy's house number, 475 Melville Place. I better let you go. You can call me when you are on the road. You should still have coverage. When I say coverage, I mean that you should still be able to make a phone call," she explained.

"I've been around my grandson long enough that I know what coverage is. Sam tells me we have little coverage at our house. I'm talking as we're walking so I won't miss our ride. We're leaving with our other neighbors, the Kurts, Martha and Ken.

"I'm not sure if you've met them. They just built a house across the way and moved in about a year ago. They're a young couple like Kelso and yourself but with children. They'll be staying with us at your sister's house. They have a baby and a two-year-old little girl, Annie. She is a sweet thing. Are you sure you want me to sit up here with Ken? OK, honey, I had better go. Is everything all right with you?"

"Yep. Love you, Dad." Penny tried to contain herself. "Tell Mom I'll talk to her soon, and I love you both."

"Try to get some sleep. It shouldn't be so bad where you're at from what I see on the news. Bye," Penny's father said as he hung up the phone.

Penny was going to say something else but realized she was just trying to keep him on the phone. She would have talked with her dad for as long as she could, but it was time to say goodbye.

Kelso was letting Kelso inside the house when he heard Penny say, 'Bye.'

"So, they've got a caravan of people heading to Nancy's house in the country? Please promise me that we will not end up there," Kelso said. He wondered if they eventually also should be headed out that way. He would dread being in close quarters with Penny's sister and a bunch of strangers. But if Penny and he would be safer. he would endure it. He shivered at the thought.

"It's not a bad idea, you know," said Penny. "It isn't near any major calamity of which we know. It looks like most of the damages from the earthquakes hit the East and West Coasts. Within the United States, there's massive flooding in Colorado and Mississippi, as well as the mile-wide tornadoes in parts of Oklahoma, but not where my sister's house is in Wyoming. It's relatively quiet. It's far away from everything, including people. Not that it is important to be that far out from civilization, unless ..." Penny snickered as she thought about her earlier mention of ancient civilizations' end-time prophecies.

Kelso looked behind him and gave her the stink eye as he turned the TV back on.

The TV aired information about the East Coast earthquakes and a major earthquake along the Mississippi fault line. It registered 7.2 on the Richter scale. Photos were shown of extensive damage done by the Mississippi earthquake that had occurred over a week ago. But as bad as it was, it didn't compare to the aftermath of the quakes up and down the West Coast. Kelso was glad they were not stranded somewhere and most people he knew were safe.

It was then that Penny and Kelso heard a big bang. The lights went off. There was a silence as they stood in darkness. "It must have been the electric company's generator that provides power for the electric power grid. Our little town may stay dark for a while." said Kelso. It was continued quiet until there was a humming sound and the lights flickered as they turned back on. Their backup generator, which was partially solar-powered, had kicked in.

"How long will our generator last?" asked Penny, so glad they weren't going to be left in the dark.

Kelso shrugged as he walked to the front door to let in the forgotten dog, who was patiently waiting for him on the front porch. He knew this dog was going to be a good dog; it seemed from his behavior that he may have already been housebroken. Jasmine and Tom knew what they were doing when it came to fostering dogs. "The house can sustain energy for a month at least or maybe more. We've never tested it, but in the long run, it will be much more expensive."

The television didn't turn on automatically, so Penny reached for the controller and turned it on but hit the mute button so she could listen to Kelso as he continued to talk.

"It's helpful that a small part of the generator's source of power can be obtained from the solar panels attached to the pergola in the backyard," he said. "I already unattached it from the hot tub. We could use the hot tub to catch the rainwater—if we ever get rain." Kelso had already drained and sterilized the tub in anticipation of using it as a cistern, although they weren't expecting much rain in the near future.

Kelso hit the mute button on the controller, and once again, there was sound from the television. Penny, who had gone to the kitchen for a glass of water, came back to the living room and joined him. She peered over his shoulder while he sat on the couch.

Pictures flashed on the television of what looked like cell phone video footage of something falling from the sky. It was part of a meteor. Then a map of the Midwest appeared as a news anchor, Michelle Brann, explained that this did not affect the outlying states and was not part of the natural phenomena that was affecting the outlying parts of America. "In other words," said Michelle, "it was not the cause for any recent recordings of seismographic activity." She continued. "The aftereffects of the meteor affected mostly the electrical and water supply for multiple surrounding states. The fallen meteor did little physical damage to the surrounding areas. Mostly the electricity will be scarcer, and the water supply may have been tainted. The major river basins, which are the sources of drinkable water for the outlying states are currently being tested. The Missouri, the Mississippi, the Green, the Colorado, the Snake, and the Columbia are being tested for acidity levels that could be considered toxic. The Great Salt Lake has not been compromised, but unfortunately only accounts for 2 percent of Wyoming's water source, mostly through filtration of condensation." Michelle fiddled with her microphone. Subtitles streamed at the bottom of the screen warning people to stay calm, to stay indoors, and to listen to the radio.

"Does anyone besides us even still have a radio?" asked Penny, who was now visibly relieved. "Mom and Dad should be fine at my sister's house. It's outside of Jackson, Wyoming. It has not only well water but also redundant septic tanks." Penny paused and added, "Because everyone needs those."

Kelso laughed.

"We should be safe too—especially since the people from which we bought this house put in more than a decent backup generator. I don't think we're going to have to join my parents in Wyoming," said Penny.

Kelso continued to watch the television screen and concentrated on the information that was being disseminated. Even though it was worse than what he'd thought could happen int the "good old US of A," other than a nuclear attack, he knew that, somehow, people would pull together and make the best of a bad situation. The government would be able to put back the pieces and restore civility to the States. As for now, he was glad that Penny had talked with her parents, which had set her heart at ease.

The bad news continued; almost everywhere it was the same—mass confusion. Many people on the East Coast were migrating west. People on the West Coast were headed east. There were countless stories of mass looting and raiding of stores and houses. But for what? Kelso asked himself.

As more reports of major fatalities across the United States flooded the news, Kelso felt his heart sink. Despite what the media was projecting—that everyone, including all of Wyoming, would feel mild ramifications from the meteor—Kelso felt in the pit of his stomach that, after some time, the world would know it to be more severe. As the sky turned red over many different cities and larger parts of states, the ecosystem would be in a state of flux, and mild ramifications would turn into major ones.

Kelso rose from the couch and entered the kitchen. Penny followed him. She opened the cupboard and took out a jar of spaghetti sauce. Kelso the dog quickly came over and sat at her feet. He looked up with his ears close to his head as if to say, *I'm guilty of begging.*

"What do you say we think of a new name for this dog?" asked Kelso, who was glad to be away from the television and doing something different.

Penny seemed a little out of it. "I guess we can," she said.

Kelso wished Penny would come back to Earth. It was times when Penny withdrew from reality when he felt the solitary weight of being Penny's husband.

"What do you think of Fido or Spot? Now those are dogs' names." Kelso, after seeing the jar of spaghetti sauce in Penny's hand, went to the refrigerator and took out some vegetables. He laid them on the counter and removed a cutting board from the cupboard. He started to cut the onions, mushrooms, and green peppers to add to the sauce.

Penny mechanically joined in and took some basil leaves from the plant next to the window and handed them to Kelso, who washed the leaves and chopped them into little pieces. Penny then retrieved dishes, silverware, and two drinking glasses from a drawer and cupboard. She set them aside on the breakfast bar across the counter, opposite of where Kelso was standing.

Kelso the dog was submissively lying on the ground whining with his head between his paws.

"How about Silver? Since he has a lot of gray, in his fur and in the light, it looks a little silver. It could be short for Quicksilver, liquid mercury? It moves quickly." Penny knew if Kelso was willing to settle on Fido or Spot he was desperate for change. Penny had been thinking on names since she Jasmine had given her the stray. But now saying it out loud, Silver seemed to fit the best.

"Sure. Anything's an improvement. I believe Silver was the Lone Ranger's horse, which is fitting, since he is a big dog, and I believe him to be a loyal companion." Kelso tried to sound like Tonto in his best Johnny Depp personation. "I don't know why Jasmine agreed to foster him as a pet since she hardly has room in that condo of hers. What did you want to add to the spaghetti sauce, sausage, hamburger, or chicken?" Kelso was truly excited that they'd found another name.

"Chicken, we need the protein without all the fat. We probably need to use up what we have and what will spoil the quickest, just in case we need to travel," said Penny. She slid next to Kelso to steal some of his vegetables for the salad she was making. Penny loved cooking in the kitchen next to Kelso. It was on her list of most romantic things to do together.

"Hey now, the sauce isn't going to taste the same without any vegetables. By the way, what does spoil the quickest?" Kelso asked as he nudged her.

Penny shrugged and smiled. She took out a cucumber, a tomato, parmesan cheese, and some hamburger from the refrigerator. She handed the hamburger to Kelso.

He knew she'd said chicken but didn't want to call her on it. He would barbecue the chicken tomorrow night for dinner. "Oh good, hamburger; you changed your mind. I like a beef sauce for spaghetti better than a chicken sauce anyway. I am just going to barbecue the chicken tomorrow night for dinner."

She realized she had gotten out the hamburger instead of the chicken. "That's what I was thinking; if we're not traveling, it's all the same." She smiled to herself at her mistake. She knew it didn't matter. Hamburger probably did spoil quicker than chicken. The amount of spoilage time was minimal, only a couple days difference between the two. Certainly, both were quicker than sausage, with all those preservatives and seasonings filtered in with the meat. Penny felt herself losing focus and reminded herself to stay on topic, which was dinner and her conversation with Kelso.

"We won't be traveling. We just need to wait this out. I'm not sure what's going on, but the dust hasn't even started to settle yet. When it does, everything will slowly get back to normal. We have to take each day as it comes and make the best of what we have. Most of all, we need to be grateful for everything," said Kelso. He hoped his words were true.

Kelso grabbed the remote for the television from the cabinet and clicked on the up arrow several times to turn up the volume. The TV news station broadcasted that the National Guard had been called out to maintain peace up and down the coast of California. People were warned not to be out passed 7:00 p.m. The National Guard would be fortified mostly in Southern California.

Both Penny and Kelso dropped what they were doing to go and sit in front of the television. Kelso doubled back to turn off the burners for the boiling pot of spaghetti and the sauce simmering in a pan beside it.

"Extreme weather and natural disasters have affected many islands and countries around the world. The Philippines wait for their third current typhoon to hit in the last two months. Meanwhile volcanos in places like Indonesia as well as the Hawaiian Islands are causing thousands to evacuate," said Michelle from the blaring television.

She continued to explain. "There are six hundred active volcanoes currently, compared to five hundred volcanoes that were active less than ten years ago. Ten of the six hundred currently active are now erupting. Some of them are only shield volcanoes, which will not cause any damage, while others can cause and are causing substantial damage." Michelle, reading from the teleprompter, continued to rattle off the different islands and places where these eruptions were taking place. "The shift in the earth's plates as well as other strange occurrences, such as breaks in the ocean floor, have been blamed for some of the natural catastrophes.

"A super volcano under Naples, Italy, is of current concern for seismologists; it's located between the earth's Eurasian and African plates. Rising temperatures and traces of sulfuric gases have increased in the last decade. Two other super-volcanoes that are active are not considered a threat. One is located in Yellowstone, USA, and the other in Indonesia. Now here is Donald with more about earthquakes." Michelle picked up her cell phone and walked off camera.

Part of the conversation could be heard over the television. Kelso and Penny had guessed that she must have been talking to her child, as she said that Mommy would be home as soon as she could and that she was trying to get someone else to cover for her.

Donald kept staring at Michelle, although she was not on camera. He smiled as he talked about the earthquakes as he tried to wave to Michelle to turn off her mic, which eventually she did. "Earthquakes are being felt throughout the world—some with a magnitude as high as 8.9, which was the same magnitude as the earthquake that shook Japan in 2011. Some tremors are as significant as 5.2, that of an average-size earthquake. Japan, at the present, seems to be the only country that is not suffering from severe weather or natural phenomenon," said Donald. "A little too far to travel wouldn't you say, Michelle?" He looked over at Michelle.

Kelso and Penny felt uneasy as the news broadcasters started to act out the consequences of the news they'd reported. The cryptic message for Michelle was not to leave the news room, as they were very shorthanded. The message was unencrypted across the nation. The camera panned over to Michelle, who was refastening her mic to her blouse.

"Much of our video footage and information is being captured from personal cameras, cell phones, and tweets. We want to thank you for keeping us and other viewers informed. Here's some footage of Great Britain's coast as it is battered by one of its worst storms in its history, with winds up to 105 miles per hour. That's equal to the gale force of a category type 2 hurricane," said Donald as he smiled at Michelle, who now returned to the television screen. Her cheeks looked a little pinker.

"Thanks, Donald. Live with us now, we have two renowned scientists, Calvin Aires, a meteorologist, who predicted some of these events in his book, *You See The Sky,* and fellow scientist and college professor, Gregor Mendel, who has several doctorates in geology. They are here to comment on why these natural phenomena may be occurring quickly and consecutively. Dr. Mantle will also explain why the magnetic force shield that usually protects the earth's atmosphere has weakened, thus explaining the asteroid debris that fell to earth in Wyoming. Here to continue this interview is Donald," said Michelle as she looked down at her blouse and took off her mic again. She looked up at the camera, shocked as she realized she was still on camera.

Donald was still shaking his head as the camera panned over to him.

Kelso got up from the couch and headed to the kitchen.

"Where are you going? Should I change the channel to another network?" asked Penny.

Kelso didn't answer.

Silver started to growl. Penny's eyes widened as she looked at Kelso. Silver raised his head and then put it back down.

"I don't know if we're better off having this dog or not. He might just scare the pants off of us," said Kelso.

Penny turned down the sound on the television and started to follow Kelso into the kitchen. "Don't get up. I can listen to the television from the kitchen. I'm getting hungry. I'll finish making dinner, and we can eat it on the couch," said Kelso.

"Are you sure you don't want my help?" asked Penny.

"No, I am sure. I'm putting the spaghetti on the plate. It's done cooking, although it is a little al dente. Now ... smothering it in sauce—not so much sauce for you. I'm taking the cottage cheese out of the refrigerator and putting a scoop of it on your plate next to your spaghetti, just how you like it. I'm now plating the salad ... opening the refrigerator and grabbing the raspberry vinaigrette," Kelso said teasingly.

"You remembered the cottage cheese.", Penny said as she places her hands over her heart. "OK, my fine husband, as you wish, I will let you wait on me." Penny loved the fact that Kelso could lighten the mood of a somber situation with just a few words. "If need be, I'll rewind this segment when you're able to sit down with me."

Silver started to softly growl again, but as before he raised his dog ears and then put his head back on the ground. Kelso, who had not recently prayed as much as he used to, prayed that there wasn't trouble on the horizon.

"I'm going to call Nancy to see how she's doing. Nancy will have more information about current affairs in the White House. That is if she can talk," Penny said, holding up her phone. Just them, it rang.

"Nance how are you?" said Penny.

"You knew it was me before you picked up the phone, didn't you, little sis? Isn't that just like you? So what is your intuition telling you about our current events?" asked Nance rhetorically.

"I was just going to call you. Since we're usually on the same page, that's how I knew it was you. Since you divinely decided to call me at the same time, couldn't it be *us* with the intuition or sixth sense, not just me? Also, you beat me to the phone call, so your intuition may kick in faster than mine," Penny added, trying to switch up the compliment.

Nancy held the phone from her ear and twisted her head a bit and smiled. "OK then, you have a way of putting things in perspective for me. The reason I'm calling you is not to check in on how you're doing. I assume you and Kelso are making the best of a bad situation. I'm calling you for a huge favor. I was hoping that you could take

Sam. Our company is consulting on a major security matter. I was asked for personally by the secretary of state because of the past work that we've done for the White House. She said, my 'extensive Middle East background' is 'important.' Anyway, there is a small airfield about fifteen minutes south of you. I believe it's the J. Brie Airfield. I would drop Sam off there."

Silver started to bark. Penny was becoming perturbed with her sister and Silver. "Can't you just leave him with Mom and Dad at your country house?" asked Penny.

Silver continued to bark as Nancy continued to talk. "I prefer Sam being with you and Kelso. Is that a dog? Did you get a dog?" Nancy asked, not waiting for an answer. "I can't believe you got a dog. Sam is going to love it. Anyway, I would be there now, but I can't leave right away. I can't talk about why, but I will be there tomorrow around noon. I will text you if I will be any later. Charge your phones tonight. Electricity is scarce in many parts of the United States right now."

Penny blankly stared at the television. "Nancy, we don't know anything about how to take care of a nine-year-old boy. What does he eat?" asked Penny.

Kelso took a seat beside Penny as he put their dinners on the coffee table.

"What does he *eat*?" exclaimed Kelso in unison with Nancy on the other end of the phone. Kelso and Nancy laughed. "Tell Nance, it's OK. We will do this," Kelso said as he grabbed Penny's hand and held it.

Silver was now at the door barking and wagging his tail. Kelso had started to get up when Penny grabbed his arm.

Her grip was small compared to his forearm. "I'm just going to check why Silver is barking," Kelso said as he continued to stand. Her phone was placed face down on her leg.

Her eyes were bigger and more beseeching than that of Silver's, a beggar by trade. "Can you wait until I get off the phone with Nancy?" asked Penny.

Kelso lifted his eyebrows and shook his head like it was no big deal as he walked toward the door.

"At least take the Glock," exclaimed Penny.

Kelso shrugged and took the gun out of the drawer of the small antique table in the foyer.

"A gun? My little sister has a gun. Keep it away from Sam, but it is probably better if you have one than not. People are going crazy out there. I mean really nuts. I'll let you go, sis. See you tomorrow and take care," said Nancy.

"Bye for now," said Penny. She put down the phone and stood next to Silver and Kelso.

Kelso listened at the front door but didn't hear anything, yet Silver was excited. He then put his hand on the doorknob and pulled opened the door. Penny screamed. Kelso started to lift his gun with his right hand and then put it down.

Jasmine screamed a little too but only as if to say, *We're here.*

Kelso, who was not the type to shoot first and ask questions later, had already recognized both Jasmine and Tom and had promptly lowered the gun to his side. He still wasn't that comfortable with a gun and quickly put it back in the drawer. He came back to the door and put his arm around Tom, Jasmine's husband, and patted him on the back. "Welcome," Kelso said.

Tom and Kelso grabbed their overnight bags and pulled them into the house.

Penny had already grabbed Jasmine before Kelso had welcomed Tom. Penny and Jasmine started hugging and swaying as if they had been separated for years. Both had tears in their eyes. They let go of each other briefly.

Silver was extremely hyper at seeing Jasmine. And although he tried not to jump up, he knocked into her, and she took a couple of steps backward onto the porch. Silver followed. Penny reached out, grabbed her friend's arm, and pulled her inside. Silver, surprisingly, did not run off but followed Jasmine into the house.

"Why didn't you call or text me?" asked Penny.

"I did. I didn't get a response. I didn't have Kelso's phone number handy, and we were in a rush to get out of town. We thought we'd be safer if we were to just drive and leave town. The condo with all its security didn't feel safe, and the lights started to flicker so we weren't sure for how much longer we would have electricity. Also, the building may not be as secure in its foundational structure as they once thought. Some of the cracks in the front of the building had one of the inspectors concerned. So, we weren't going to wait to find out and have to vacate," said Jasmine.

Tom joined in. "We weren't going to stay with you, but the more we drove, the closer we came to your house. We realized that we had no other place to go, so we took a chance on your place. We weren't even sure you'd be here." Tom looked relieved. "It's nuts out there. I could go for a beer. Do you have any?" He looked at Kelso, who did not drink.

Kelso wondered if they had any beer in their refrigerator out in the garage and got up to check but returned empty-handed.

"Many places up and down the coast are without electricity. We also weren't sure about the safety of the motels or hotels. Plus, most five- or four-star hotels that we accessed online or while we were driving past didn't have availability or were just turning people away. It seems that everyone is looking for a safe place to lay their heads. I have a couple of secure backup places we could go as a last resort that would work for all of us if necessary, but we thought we would play it by ear. It seems like this area is doing OK." As Jasmine said this, she gave her husband a glance to let him know they'd made the right choice. "And you were our first choice," she added. It was more eloquently said than the way Tom had explained it.

Tom went and stood next to Jasmine. "We parked down the road in case we were being followed. It's far from normal out there. On our way here, after wading through major traffic on most of the thoroughfares, we noticed cars just parked along some of the side roads. People were camped out with their families alongside their cars. We were frightened for them, as we thought about the possibility of carjacking. There was a warning on the radio for people to stay in their cars and not to vacate their vehicles on the highways—also to be on alert for criminals looting gas stations and stores, as well as committing carjacking. There was a reminder that these acts are felonies. There's a number to call, which Jasmine wrote down," he said.

Jasmine picked up her phone and texted the shared contact information to Penny, slid her phone back into her pocket, and smiled.

"We left shortly after you had left our condominium with our foster dog, and we're just now getting here. Sorry if we startled you," said Tom. He reached down and patted Silver's head.

"I'm just glad you're here. Do we need to get your things out of the car? Or is this all of it?" asked Penny.

"No, that's not all of it. Kelso and I will go get the rest of our things," said Tom with a take-charge attitude.

"It's dark out there. Why don't you wait until tomorrow morning? said Penny in an authoritative tone of her own.

Jasmine agreed. "We have our overnight bags," she said. "It should be all right."

"I think it will be fine if we go and come back. If there's anything suspicious, we should be able to spot it. I think the best bet is securing your possessions. It should be a short run or walk. Did you say it was about a mile down the road?" said Kelso.

"I didn't say, but that would be about right. I agree. If we leave it until morning, there's a possibility there won't be too much left of our stuff. We brought about as much as we could to the door with us, but there are still some things with which I would not like to part, like our wedding album," said Tom.

Jasmine's eyes caught his and smiled. She nodded in agreement.

"We all should go. Jasmine and I will follow with Silver. Kelso you can carry the gun in your pants. Just don't shoot anything down there," said Penny and laughed with a little snort. She amused herself with her jokes, but no one laughed, not even a snicker.

Penny was trying to be logical and safe with regards to the gun. Kelso had felt the same way up until the point when the gun become a necessity. He hated the darn thing as soon as he pulled it from their antique table. The romanticized notion of owning a gun was in the past. Something told him he would not need it, and it would become more of a hassle if he had to always take it with him. It wasn't that he was worried about it accidentally going off, but rather he had to keep it with him just in case.

He also wished there did not have to be a group discussion about everything—that was planned. He and Tom could have been to the car and back by now.

Timing and protection were at the forefront of Kelso's thinking. "OK, but we don't bring Silver. If there are carjackers out there, it's only one more step up to becoming a house jacker. And Silver needs to protect the house if no one will be here. Leave him," said Kelso.

Penny looked at Jasmine and frowned; the dog was their only means of protection. Jasmine had no concerns about Tom going to the car. She only had concerns about others being concerned. Jasmine's eyes rolled to the side. She looked at Tom as if this trip to the car was getting out of hand. Tom met Jasmine's eyes with a look of understanding. He shook his head no at Jasmine.

"No, Kelso and I will go and be back. It will take only

two of us to bring back our stuff. Just hold tight. Kelso, do you have a flashlight?" asked Tom.

Kelso was already ahead of him. He had put on his light jacket. He then opened the drawer that held the Glock 42, slid it into the back of his pants, and took out two pocket flashlights from within the same drawer and handed one of them to Tom.

"You have your running shoes on?" Kelso asked rhetorically as he opened the front door. As they stepped out the front door Kelso explained the plan. "I know a path by the road we can take until we spot your car. We should be able to hear or see if anyone is on the path, since it's pretty straight. But keep your eyes open, and I'll do the same. Also, if we run into anyone that's questionable, I don't plan on being a hero. I'll tell you that right now. We run the other way. I don't use the gun for any reason other than self-defense. If your car is being vandalized, we don't shout, 'What the hell are you doing?' We just make tail and get the hell out of there. Got it?!"

"You're the boss, Boss. We really appreciate this, Kelso," said Tom.

Kelso nodded at Tom and signaled forward with his right hand as if he was now a 3D player in *Call of Duty*. "Let's go!"

Kelso, who had already broken into a sprint, came to a dead stop to put his hand on Tom's chest. Tom, who was ex-military. was not used to anyone putting their hands on his chest, but he took pride in the fact that he had changed in this manner.

"One more thing—no more words," Kelso said.

He started to sprint again. He circled around the

house not to come straight down their rocky driveway and tried to see if there were any vagrants hanging around their yard or the entrance to their house. It was the first time he was happy that their house could not be readily seen from the road.

Most every party Penny and he had hosted had inevitably at least one or more invitees who had missed the driveway and couldn't find the house. Sometimes after missing the driveway, the would-be guests decided to just go home.

Kelso looked down the road before making his way to the dirt path. There were no cars immediately parked within a half-mile vicinity west of their house.

Tom and Kelso connected with the path that ran parallel to the road within a couple of minutes. They had only traveled a mile when they started to see cars and stragglers along the side of the road. He was glad that Tom knew better than to say what when he pointed at them. They kept their flashlights in their pockets for the time being.

After traversing a mile and a half up the path, they spotted Jasmine and Tom's car. They also spotted a car to the right and left of Tom's car. The cars were on the other side of the road headed away from their house, which Kelso thought was odd because that way was not headed out of town but into town. He reminded himself to focus on the task at hand.

The smell of onions and spaghetti sauce permeated the air. "Would you like some spaghetti?" asked Penny.

Jasmine saw the plates and waters set on the coffee table in front of the television. "Starving, do you mind?", Jasmine said as Penny made room on the couch and Jasmine switched seats and sat beside her. They sat together and watched the news as the newscasters reported around the world on the bizarre weather events and natural catastrophes that had occurred. They ate their spaghetti without saying a word, engulfed in every picture and word that was blasted through the television. Subtitles gave information on where to go in an emergency and numbers to call or text, and the warning to remain calm at all times appeared in bold type at the bottom of the screen.

"Do you have any more spaghetti I can make? When do you think our men are going to be home? I wouldn't mind if we went looking for them. After all, that was your suggestion—that we would go with them. I also think if we took Silver with us, we could let him go and attack whoever if we felt threatened. I think the house will be safe enough with or without Silver. Great name by the way—Silver instead of Kelso!" said Jasmine.

Jasmine wasn't concerned about their safety but, rather, about Penny feeling threatened and scared for Kelso. Jasmine knew she could handle any threat that came their way in the dark for the two of them, the same as Tom could handle getting their bags. But because Jasmine was especially good at reading people and could tell that Penny was worried, she again volunteered to venture out.

"Tom and Kelso will be fine," said Penny, as if Jasmine was the woman who was nervously biting her index fingernail. "We will give them at least another fifteen minutes. I'll get you that spaghetti," said Penny as if she had totally dismissed the idea. "We definitely shouldn't take Silver. I'm not sure if we let him go who he would attack. Silver may just go after Kelso. He doesn't know us that well, yet. Hopefully over time," she added.

Jasmine agreed.

Penny got up to get the two of them more spaghetti and to put some of the sauce in the refrigerator to save for later.

"Tom don't do anything until I tell you the coast is clear," said Kelso.

They stayed still for what seemed like hours but was only a few minutes. Tom tried to see if there were any people in the parked cars. If there were, they were slouched down in their cars. Or they were somewhere else.

Finally, Kelso saw someone. "Do you see that person on the passenger side of your car? Actually, I think there are two people," said Kelso.

At that moment, Tom's head shot up. He looked at Kelso and then looked back at his car. Tom's military background took over. When it came to fight or flight, he chose fight, totally forgetting his and Kelso's plan.

"Hey, what the hell are you doing with my car, you sons of bitches? I have a gun, and I'm not afraid to use it." Tom made his way out of hiding and down the hill from the path they were on. Kelso tackled his legs, and he fell face forward onto the ground.

"What did we talk about, you bastard? Run!" exclaimed Kelso in a loud whisper. They still had enough of a distance to make it back safely to their house without being followed.

It was as if Tom had just gotten his memory back. Kelso looked at Tom's face as he had whispered in his ear. Tom's eyes were huge and apologetic. "I'm sorry, man. I forgot."

"Are you OK? What's all that commotion?" came a woman's voice from below, concerned now about the rustling from above. "You don't have to shoot us. We just live up the street and heard that people were camping in their cars or just roughing it outside instead of staying in the city. We just wanted to open up our home to anyone who needs a place to stay. It can get pretty cold at night sometimes."

"Tom, it's not bad enough you curse at them but you are going to shoot them, too? No brownies for you," said Kelso, laughing as he helped Tom to his feet. Once on them, Tom pushed Kelso in the other direction, causing him to lose his balance. They made their way down the hill to the couple who stood by the car.

"I'm Jag and this is my wife, Beverly," said the husband.

Tom used his key fob to unlock his car. He ignored the two neighbors and started to unload his and Jasmine's stuff from the trunk of the car, while Kelso spoke with the couple. Kelso recognized the couple from his weekend late-morning runs. They were usually in their front yard gardening.

"Do you know where the people from these other two cars are?" Kelso asked.

Beverly pointed to an electric Prius and said that one was theirs.

"Were you successful? Did you find any drifters, people who are looking for a place to stay?" asked Kelso.

"No. We couldn't find anyone who was still in their cars. We came across five cars in total, not including ours. I think the three cars that were across the road from us are guests of our neighbors, the Kilkenny's. At least we recognize the cars. They've been parked there on several other occasions," said Beverly.

Tom approached the couple and set down three bags beside Kelso. Tom had stuffed everything from the middle and front seat of the car into the three large bags. "What's your phone number?" Tom asked Jag.

Overcome with excitement, Beverley quickly pulled out her phone and showed it to Jag and made an embarrassed face. Her phone didn't have any charge left. Kelso wasn't sure why she couldn't just tell him the number and had to pull out her phone, but it was inconsequential.

As Jag told him what their cell number was, Tom dialed it. "OK. Now you have my number. It's the last number that called you. If there's any trouble, don't hesitate to call me. Go home and don't try to pick up vagrants. There have been reports of car heists up and down the highways. Keep your phone charged in case of an emergency. Take care," said Tom as he slapped his hand on Kelso's back.

Beverly and Jag nodded in agreement. Kelso knelt

down and picked up two of the bags and left the largest, overstuffed bag for Tom to take.

Beverly was thankful they had run into Kelso and Tom. "Would you two men like to have dinner with us? Or have you eaten?" blurted out Beverly.

Jag didn't mind her impromptu invitations. He was used to it, and in turn, he was grateful for all his impromptu dinner parties and guests, for which she was always prepared. Jag grabbed her hand and waited for their response.

"No thanks. But thank you for offering. We have dinner waiting at home," said Kelso but thought he might skip dinner and just go to bed. "It was nice finally meeting you two," he added.

They made their way up the hill to the path. They turned to watch the couple make their way to their car and climb in after unlocking the car. In silence, the eco-friendly car drove away.

"It is amazing how quiet those electric vehicles can be. Where do you think the driver from this classic is?" asked Kelso as he walked past the car that faced eastward. He also wondered why the driver of the car had turned the Plymouth around so that it was parked in the direction of ongoing traffic. He would check and see if the vehicle was still there in the morning.

Tom made a mental note of the license plate.

They quickly walked home with their bags partially on their backs as they listened for voices but heard none. This was the most exhausted Kelso had been in a very long time. He could not wait to crawl into his bed next to his beautiful wife. He was thankful that Tom and Jasmine had decided not to brave it in the city. He knew this was just the beginning of many exhausting days.

As Tom and Kelso approached the door, they heard Silver barking. Kelso had to remind himself that they had a dog now. He had already grown attached to Silver, who seemed to be a great dog. Luckily, they had a large yard, two acres of property in which Silver could run and play. The front yard was partially fenced, so they wouldn't have to worry about Silver roaming the neighborhood. It had never occurred to Kelso or Penny to adopt a dog because of the dual-income couple's time constraints.

Penny quickly opened the door to let Tom and Kelso in from the dark. Jasmine and Penny had been watching them jump the fence and walk up the front yard from the side and front window.

Silver jumped up on Kelso. Kelso set the bags down in the foyer and petted Silver around the ears and head. As he stood up, he gave Penny a kiss. He pulled the gun from his pants and placed it back into the drawer.

"How was it?" asked Jasmine.

"It was fine," said Tom.

"Looks like you have some scratches and maybe what will be a bruise on your face. Did you get into a fight with someone or just trip?" asked Jasmine.

Kelso shut and bolted the door behind him and drew the blinds and curtains in the front window. Kelso was no longer mad at Tom for forgetting about their agreement to run at the first sign of trouble. He was just looking forward to sleep.

"No … not a fight. I just fell," said Tom as he looked

over at Kelso, who had tackled him. Kelso's cheeks turned partially crimson.

Kelso put his hand on his shoulder. "How about that cold beer? Let me see what I have." He'd remembered one beer tucked away in the bottom of the kitchen refrigerator.

"Actually, I'll settle for forty winks," said Tom.

Penny was in the kitchen preparing two large bowls of pasta. She and Jasmine had eaten all of the spaghetti noodles that she and Kelso and had prepared earlier, so she quickly put some angel hair pasta in the boiling water. She was glad she had it on hand, since it cooked more quickly than regular spaghetti noodles.

Penny loved their house; the owners who had been the architects of the house had considered the same nuances important that she and Kelso would have if they had built their own house. She loved the griddle that was built in to the stovetop, which she used for almost everything, from pancakes to grilled cheeses. The fact that they had gas instead of electric was also preferred. Gas stoves heated up water much faster than electric, which tonight came in handy. She also felt validated on having bought their home that was 10 percent over the asking price.

Penny always tried to have a positive attitude. There were enough negative and cynical people around her that she was always happy to come into contact with another individual who had a cheery outlook. Positive thoughts of being grateful took her away from the normal daily stresses she, from time to time, could obsess over. Penny had quickly latched on to Jasmine when they first met.

Jasmine was both mostly positive and, at the same time, seemed to keep a wary eye on those around her, never expecting the best of anyone. Penny knew she had a different side that she kept hidden. Jasmine had told her that she'd almost become a bitter and caustic person at one point in her life, but she was not that same person now. It took Penny at least a year to learn she needed to take Jasmine at face value and not to probe into some of the comments she made. Penny's thoughts quickly turned from Jasmine back to spaghetti and her current task at hand.

Penny needed to feed her husband soon. Kelso would insist on going to bed without eating if it was too late in the evening. He always would forgo the extra calories if he could, but sometimes he would wake up in the middle of the night famished and go into the kitchen and eat an excessive number of calories. She pulled the noodles off of the stovetop and poured it into the colander that was left in the kitchen sink from their previous batch of noodles.

Penny looked up from the kitchen sink through window in front of her and saw a flash of light. She leaned closer into the window and looked again, straining her eyes to see anything but saw nothing. She waited a few moments and still saw nothing. *Wouldn't Silver bark if there was someone out there?* She guessed. If she told Kelso, he would want to investigate, and it was late. She would rather have him to herself, home safe.

Penny, like her husband, was looking forward to the day ending. She just wanted to lose herself to perfect sleep, instead of all the thoughts of impending doom that swirled within her young brain. Penny knew she would wait for this day and perhaps these next few months to pass before she would try to make sense of all the crap that was happening.

Just as she had held on to Kelso's words of comfort earlier that day, she once again chose these words: *This too shall pass*. It eased her mind, taking her away from being anxious. She held onto his words of encouragement, like she was in the habit of doing. Although she knew he took much of his phrases from scripture, she wasn't sure of the source of this proverb; but along with many of the things he just knew and said, she treasured it in her heart.

*It was probably nothing*, she told herself as she strained her eyes again to see out the window.

She poured the noodles in the two bowls she'd set out and left the rest of the noodles in the colander. She then poured a little bit of extra virgin olive oil on top of the noodles. She grabbed the sea salt grinder from the windowsill.

There it was again—a flash of light. But just as quickly as it had the first time, it disappeared. *Aliens*, she thought to herself. That's what was causing all the commotion around the world. They had entered the earth's atmosphere, setting everything off kilter, and the flashes of light were the aliens taking over. She couldn't stand it anymore. "Kelso, I think I see something in the backyard. There was a light. It appeared twice," Penny exclaimed.

Tom, Jasmine, and Kelso sprinted to the back window beside the sunroom. They all stood peering into the darkness. "I don't see anything," said Kelso. They continued to wait a few minutes more. "If it was a flashlight, we would see it. I don't think we need to worry. Silver would be going crazy if there was anyone out there, like he did when Jasmine and Tom arrived."

Silver was beside Kelso wagging his tail.

"I'll let him out in front, just in case, and watch him for a little while to see if he picks up on anything. I'm sure he has to go out anyway."

Penny had taken the leftover sauce from the microwave and poured it onto the two bowls of spaghetti. She took a glass from the counter, filled it with tap water from the fridge, and handed it to Tom, who was now standing in the kitchen with her. "Here, Tom, eat," she said as she next handed him the bowl of spaghetti.

Penny turned back around and opened the refrigerator and pulled out the salad from earlier and laid it on the counter. "You can help yourself to the salad as well if you would like. The dressings are in the fridge." Penny then opened the silverware drawer and took out the salad tongs and placed them in the salad. She picked up the other bowl of spaghetti, grabbed another fork, and shut the drawer. She grabbed a napkin from the napkin holder on the counter and headed toward the front of the house. She proceeded out the front door to meet Kelso.

Kelso stood on the front steps of the porch with his arms folded, watching Silver sniff the ground.

"Thanks," he said as he retrieved the bowl and fork from Penny's hands. "I don't think there's anything out there, or Silver would have picked up on it by now. Even if there was someone trespassing on our property, it's not likely that he would mean to cause us harm. Apparently, every good soul is migrating from the city to any place that's rural enough to avoid the mass hysteria and the confusion," he concluded unconvincingly.

Penny was silent as Kelso finished his bowl of spaghetti within minutes.

"Spaghetti never tasted so good.", said Kelso as he handed his bowl back to Penny. Penny made a face as if to say, *Do your own damn dishes.* But Kelso didn't notice.

"Come, Silver," Kelso said, with no response from Silver. "Come dog, come," he said a little louder. He refused to call the dog by his original name. Finally, Silver looked around and galloped up the steps and onto the porch.

Kelso, Penny. and Silver went inside.

Outside, there were two hushed voices from behind the fence. "They finally went inside. Do think they noticed us or our flashlights?" said a man with a New York accent.

"No, I don't think so, or they would have come looking for us with that dog," said the other voice.

"Great. Tomorrow we can see what valuables they have. We'll be able to use the loot for trading or maybe find a pawn shop that isn't being monitored by authorities. I'm sure they 'll be leaving the house eventually. Remember, we're not going to harm anyone unless we have to defend ourselves. One of them has a gun." said the man with the New York accent.

"Yeah, I know.", said the other voice, who hated being treated like he was the dumb one who had to have everything explained to him. "I'm just not sure about this. They seem like a nice couple."

Jasmine and Tom had already found their way to the guest bedroom with their bags. "We recently change the linens, so everything should be fresh." Penny was reflecting on the previous week when the cleaning service had been there. "If you need extra linens, there are some in the bathroom closet. Other than that, Kelso and I are only a knock away. Can you think of anything else you might need?"

"Just a good night's sleep. Love you, Pen. And thanks again for letting us stay with you guys," said Jasmine.

Tom said good night as well.

Penny could hear Jasmine and Tom talk as Jasmine closed their bedroom door. Penny listened as Jasmine and Tom prayed within the confines of their bedroom walls. It sounded as if they asked God for help and thanked Him for His protection.

Penny went and found Kelso in their bedroom starting his nightly ritual. "Maybe we should pray?" asked Penny.

Kelso just looked at his wife and said nothing. He didn't know what to say. He only supposed Penny wanted to understand what neither of them did—where was God in all of this?

Kelso was not sure they would receive the answers they sought, but he knew the best things in life sometimes began with a prayer. He looked over at his beautiful wife, nodded, and smiled. "Sure, we can pray," he said as he grabbed Penny's hand.

They prayed together and said amen.

"Let's get a good night's sleep," said Kelso as he squeezed her hand for a few seconds and let go. Kelso had long abandoned the hope that they would pray together, since she was agnostic and he was Christian, but it felt good to pray with his wife.

Kelso finished brushing his teeth. He climbed into his new striped pajamas that Penny had bought for him last weekend. He found them quite comfy. He looked at the clock; it was 10:30 p.m. He was hoping there would not be any more interruptions to an already long day.

Penny, who took much less time to get ready, was already in bed and looking at one of her world news magazines. She was much too excited to read any articles, so she just skimmed over the headlines and some of the sentences for a brief overview. But nothing was sinking in. All she could think about were the current events at hand. Martial law was a reality, and her travel options may become limited. They had to face new dangers. The more her thoughts cycled about the day's events, the more frightened she became. She looked at Kelso, who now joined her and was reading one of his running magazines. She decided not to tell him how anxious she had become.

Penny remembered something that could help calm her nerves, although she knew it could be considered silly. She popped out of bed. "I'll be right back. I need to get something out of the kitchen." She recalled what she'd picked up earlier that afternoon at a convenience store.

Penny went to the kitchen where her purse lay on one of the back counters and retrieved out of a pocket within her purse a small figurine of St. Andrew, guardian of the saints and also a cross. She shoved them in her pocket and grabbed a banana from the bowl of fruit setting on the counter and went back to bed.

Penny climbed into bed with a mouth full of banana. She raised the banana to show Kelso what she had taken from the kitchen. She grinned the type of smile that Garfield the cat would have in one of his cartoons. At that moment, she felt a little sneaky.

She was not sure she whether she would wait until Kelso fell asleep to put one of her trinkets somewhere in the room or under his pillow. Whatever she was going to do, she needed to do it before she fell asleep herself. She looked around the room as to where the best place would be to put St. Andrew.

Penny casually strolled to the window and lay the figurine against the window.

"What are you doing?" asked Kelso.

"I'm not doing anything," said Penny.

"Not doing anything looks like what I'm doing.", said Kelso as he raised his running magazine. *Whatever Penny' doing, it didn't really matter,* he thought to himself. *If she needs a private moment by the window, that's fine. But she sure looked guilty.* Then a smile came to his face. He knew what she was doing; she probably had to pass gas and didn't want to do it beside him.

"Are we reading or sleeping?" asked Kelso as Penny slid into bed next to him.

"I guess sleeping."

Kelso put his magazine down on his nightstand. Penny cozied up beside him and put her head on his pillow and pulled the blankets up over her shoulders.

Kelso then did the same, taking another pillow beside the bed and placing it under his head. He flipped over to see Penny's face too close to his and gave her a kiss on her lips as he pulled her closer to him. She smiled but wouldn't open her eyes. It was her way of saying it had been a long day. He knew he would sleep perfectly, except for the momentary need for affection, but he wasn't sure about Penny.

Penny couldn't fall asleep quickly. She flipped over unto her own pillow. It was her basic instinct to worry that took over her brain. Life for her, at this point, was overwhelming. Her thoughts would not turn off for the night. Finally, she clutched her cross in her right hand and slightly lifted it up in acknowledgement of something. She then turned on her stomach and buried her face in her pillow; still holding her cross, she eventually fell asleep.

# Chapter 2

## The Neighbors

Penny and Kelso woke up early the next morning at 5:00 a.m. Penny put on her running shoes, pants, and jacket and plugged in her earbuds.

"Can you wait for me?", Kelso asked as his feet hit the floor.

His bedhead was laughable, but Penny didn't laugh. "When was the last time that you ran more than a few miles?" she asked.

"It's been a few weeks since I went for a run that was over four miles," said Kelso.

"I guess I can go slow," said Penny teasingly.

"Hmm," Kelso said as he laced up.

"You've been taking it easy for a while. Is everything all right?" Penny asked.

"As far as I know. I have been feeling a little run-down. Anyway, running will give us a good chance to scout things out on our street," said Kelso.

"Now I know the real reason for your request to go running with me; you just want to keep an eye on me. You're worried that something's out there—something scary, something that goes bump in the night or something from the grave that is clawing it way up from the depth of hell," Penny said.

Kelso stared at Penny. He had forgotten what a morning personality she had. He chuckled and put his finger on his nose.

Jasmine and Tom were still sleeping. Penny left a note on the counter explaining that they had gone for a run and to help themselves to anything in the refrigerator. Penny hoped she and Kelso would be back before they woke so she could make them breakfast. She also wrote in the note that, if they weren't back by 7:30 a.m., someone should try to call them on either of their cell phones to make sure they were safe. She left a brief description and the map of the route she and Kelso intended to take. Although Penny knew it was overkill, the note was in the tune of "better safe than sorry."

"Can we go now? We should leave Silver for Tom and Jasmine. I've already fed him. Put that in the note. Hopefully, he won't get into anything or tear anything up while we're gone. You can walk him when we get back while I shower, or after my shower, I'll walk him," Kelso said.

Penny nodded as they headed out the front door for a brisk run.

It was still dark out. Kelso had reflective vests for both him and Penny, since they planned on running alongside the road. They decided to run a mile west down the road and then two miles back to where the cars were parked. In total it would be a decent distance, almost five miles.

The first mile up and back was clear of any stranded vehicles. Any cars that had been parked overnight were no longer on the roadside. In the other direction, they spotted the same cars Kelso and Tom had come across the previous night. They went up a little farther and saw the cars that were parked in front of Beverly's neighbor's house. Everything looked normal for their neighborhood except for the one car that was unaccounted for by any motorist, which Kelso found suspicious. It was parked facing eastward. There were no signs of the driver anywhere.

Penny and Kelso decided to climb the hill and take the path that ran alongside the road. As they climbed, the hill they noticed two people coming toward them. "Penny, come this way," said Kelso as they started to go back down the hill.

The two men came closer.

"Is this your car?" Kelso yelled up the hill. He pointed to the Plymouth sedan that was turned eastward, going into town.

The two men walked quickly down the hill, trying to catch their balance. "Yeah, this is my car. You have a problem with it?" said a short, balding man with a New York accent. He realized he was calling attention to himself and decided to take a more amicable attitude. "Where are my manners? Hi. I'm Brian Marvin. This is my friend Lou Cypher. We're not from around these parts as you can probably tell by our accents. Anyone got a quarter?" he added to make fun of his own accent. "Not that I'm asking you fellas for money or anything. A quarter ain't much."

Penny was waiting for the drumroll and the cymbal to clash.

"We were just looking for a place to stay other than the city, so we decided to camp out in these woods," said Brian.

Kelso immediately noticed that they had no camping gear or belongings other than a familiar blanket and an outdated hemp backpack. Kelso also noticed that Brian seemed a little offbeat, as if he was anxious about something or someone.

Kelso looked at Penny and raised his eyebrow.

Brian turned his attention to Lou. He looked up at Lou, who was much taller than him by at least ten inches. Lou's face had turned red.

"Dang it, Brianna. Or can I call you by your real name, Clyde! I hate that you always treat me like I'm the dumb one. If you're going to make up names you had better give me a better one than Lucifer." He fished his car keys from his pocket and walked to the car, still red in the face.

"Hey, come on Barnie. Wait for me. I didn't mean anything by it. I just thought you would think it was funny; that's all. You know your mom says Lucifer was an angel before he fell from heaven."

Clyde now turned his attention to Penny and Kelso, who were standing in front of him. "Hey fellas, I got to go, but it was a pleasure meeting you. I am glad …" Clyde said but did not finish his last sentence. He sidestepped his way to the passenger's side of the car.

Barnie peered over his shoulder at Penny and Kelso, his fair skin still red. "I'll have you know that Clyde was thinking of robbing your home if it weren't for your dog. I don't think I would have gone through with it. You need to watch yourselves. Times are changing quickly. I mean, we didn't take anything except for the blanket. It was left outside. It may not even be yours. Anyway, sorry," said

Barnie as he opened the driver side door and sat down behind the steering wheel.

Clyde, who was now buckled and sat in the front seat, had his hands against his head. After hearing Barnie's confession he lifted his head and looked through the window at Kelso and Penny. His face was expressionless, but his eyes bulging and his smile now upside down. "Barnie, you got to be kidding me. They can still get your license plate and report us to the cops. Step on it," said Clyde.

Barnie tried to start the car but it would not turn over. He tried it again and it started. He looked over at Kelso and Penny and put his hand up next to his head, waved, and smiled a crooked smile as if they were friends.

Kelso did not know how to respond. He looked down at the ground and shook his head in disbelief. Kelso and Penny sat down on the street and watched the two men drive away. The car sped off, but their loud voices were heard in the distance.

Penny's hand was firmly gripped in Kelso's on top of the pavement. "Should I have gotten the license plate number?", Penny asked. "That was a little strange, Barnie and Clyde?" Her voice cracked as she asked the question and she started to chuckle.

"No need," said Kelso. He handed Penny his water bottle. "I got it last night. Barnie and Clyde, who would have thought? I don't know why they would use fake names; their given names are hysterical. I am not sure if I was a Clyde I would ever hang out with a Barnie or date a Bonnie, but I cannot say that the names didn't suit them." He also started to chuckle.

"Do you think it ever clicked with them that their names are so cliché? Do you think it was intentional to hide their real names? Because it didn't sound like it?" said Penny.

"I don't think so. They didn't seem like they're that clever. Those were their real names. I'm sure. They just got caught," said Kelso.

"Hopefully, they learned a lesson. It sounds like Barnie was not the Bonnie type after all. He was a little mad at Clyde," said Penny, whose eyes started to tear as she laughed. They both now laughed as they sat on the pavement.

Kelso let go of Penny's hand and started squatting and stretching while they talked. Penny, with her knees in front of her and her arms behind her, got up and started to do the same. They made fun of the would-be robbers as they stretched until their laughter died down.

Penny knew she would be alarmed later when she thought about the New Yorkers' behavior and their missing blanket—the blanket that they had kept outside somewhere near the patio furniture. At the current moment, the need for laughter outweighed the current threat. It seemed to her as if it was something she would have watched on late-night oldies show. Laurel and Hardy came to mind, and she squeezed Kelso's knee and used it to push herself up, putting Kelso off balance.

"Should we report them?", asked Penny.

"They were harmless enough, but I might send an email to one of my buddies at the police department to let him know what's up. I do think this is a warning of things yet to come. We need to be careful of what goes on unnoticed around us. They had their eyes set on our house even with house guests and a dog," said Kelso in a somber voice.

"I guess we should head back home and let Jasmine and Tom know that our perimeter is secure, but not as secure as we thought," said Penny, who was now on her feet. She held out her hand to Kelso.

"Since we finished stretching, do you mind if we walk?" asked Kelso.

Penny nodded.

"I'm not feeling so great," Kelso said.

"You do look a little pale, and your face is a little swollen, like you're retaining water. It looked swollen to me the other day, but I forgot to say something. I think we were out with friends. Anyway, let me feel you lymph nodes. Is it sensitive?" Penny asked as she put both her hands on Kelso's neck.

"Yes, a little," said Kelso. "After we pick up Samuel today, I might brave the town and go see Dr. Edge. I might have to. My stomach hurts as well."

"I was going to guess a sinus infection with the puffy face, but with your stomach hurting, I'm not so sure," said Penny. Penny was quiet for a minimum of forty-five seconds before she decided to speak again. "You think you have the flu coupled with the mumps?", Penny deliberated over his symptoms. She immediately realized how stupid she sounded and thought about being quiet until her next thought popped into her head. "Oh I know, you might have mononucleosis. You can rupture your spleen, which could account for the ache," said Penny excitedly like she had solved a riddle. "When I think of how tired you've been, it's logical. It's probably why you haven't been running longer distances on your runs for the last few weeks."

"Hey, slow down on your diagnosis. You'll have me dead and buried before the doctor can get a word in edgewise. I need to get checked out before you firm up your diagnosis. If it does end up that it's mononucleosis, you need to get your blood tested as well. I'm not sure if it's only by blood that they're able to tell if the virus is present. But you should be tested, especially since they call it the 'kissing disease' and there is no one else I love to passionately kiss," said Kelso cheekily.

"I could have given it to you. But then again, I don't have any of the symptoms," said Penny. She was still deep in thought about the diagnosis. She paused and said, "I love you, too."

Penny and Kelso walked slowly back to the house. Kelso was now holding his side and sweating as he talked to Dr. Edge. Dr. Edge had been their family physician since Kelso and Penny were married and purchased their current home. "Do I call an ambulance? Really, it would take that long?" asked Kelso as he looked at Penny. "On the scale of one to ten, it's about an eight. It feels like someone is squeezing my insides. I'm not sure if I have a fever."

Penny reached out and put her hand on his forehead. She raised her eyebrows, widened her eyes, nodded, and frowned.

"I might be a little warm. I can—if you think that it's best. I'll map it out and meet you when I get there," said Kelso. The doctor continued to talk. "Got it. Yes, fine, yes. OK, got it. I will. Thanks Dr. Edge." Kelso was ready to hang up but wondered if Dr. Edge would be able to make it in time. "Is there anyone I should ask for in specific in case you do get held up? All right then, I will see you shortly."

"What would take that long?" Penny repeated Kelso's question to the doctor.

"Dr. Edge said that the hospitals are in flex. The main hospital is packed with people and doesn't have rooms or beds for everyone. And yet, the hospital is still taking transport patients from another hospital that had its ER and ICU wings damaged during the earthquake. That hospital is an hour southeast of here, near Bakersfield. That's the hospital where Dr. Edge wants us to meet and to which I will be admitted," said Kelso.

Kelso put his hand on Penny's head and pulled it close to his mouth and kissed it. "It's inconvenient; I know. I'll map it on my phone's GPS and get going. That way, I can be back sooner than later. I need you to meet your sister and pick up Sam with Jasmine. Tom needs to drive me to the hospital," said Kelso.

Kelso looked to connect with Penny, but she had started to do whatever she did inside her head to process the doctor's information and what Kelso was telling her. She couldn't bring herself to make eye contact with him yet since she hadn't yet come up with a better plan that would involve them sticking together. She was quiet for a couple of minutes and then looked at Kelso's pale face and put the back of her hand on his cheek. Her eyes started to tear up, but she blinked a couple times to keep herself from crying. She thought something could be seriously wrong.

"If you think it's best that Tom takes you, but they could pick Sam up instead of me," said Penny. Essentially the hardest information for Penny to process was that Kelso was going to the hospital without her.

Kelso knew Penny's reservations translated to, *I am going to come up with another plan and tell you about it before you get out the door so I can be with you.*

Silver was barking as they walked up the steps. Jasmine was telling Silver to be quiet and not to bark. As they opened the door, they were overwhelmed with the smells of breakfast. Tom and Jasmine had made frittatas, Virginia ham, and pancakes, and fresh cut fruit was waiting on the table. Jasmine and Tom would wait to eat until after they had gone for their run, but they thought it would be nice to have something ready for Penny and Kelso when they came back. Jasmine wasn't much of a cook, but Tom was. He had done most of the preparation, along with the frittatas, ham, and pancakes. Unfortunately, he was not good with portions and cooked enough for eight people instead of four.

"Hey, Tom, would you mind driving me to the hospital? I have appendicitis or perhaps something else." He looked at Penny. "Maybe mono, so it could be my spleen that hurts. Anyway, we have to go now," said Kelso.

"That's awful. Tom would be glad to drive. Is there anything else we can do?" Jasmine asked. Tom was looking bewildered as he reached for his running jacket on the chair.

"Do I have time to change out of my running clothes?", asked Tom.

Jasmine shook her head no, and she quickly got up and darted into their room. She picked out an outfit for him and stuffed it into a gym bag, along with some miscellaneous items. They were already in the driveway when she caught up with them. Tom had a pancake sandwich stuffed with frittata and ham surrounded by fruit in a Tupperware dish beside him in the driver's seat.

Jasmine looked at her husband in bewilderment. Tom always seemed to make the best of any situation. She had developed an appreciation of his easygoing manner over the years they had been married and hoped some of it would eventually rub off on her. Tom smugly smiled at his wife and his concoction. Jasmine handed Tom the gym bag, which he tossed over his shoulder and into the back seat.

"Keep us posted, and I'm praying for you both. Godspeed, Kelso," said Jasmine. It sounded like a directive, as if she had a premonition of what difficulties they would encounter. She stuck her head in the car and gave Tom a quick kiss goodbye.

"I appreciate that. Take care of Penny. She is a little, well you know, distraught. Also you need to pick up her sister's kid if we, or Tom, are not back by noon," said Kelso.

"Will do," said Jasmine with a little salute to Kelso and Tom.

Tom saluted back and winked. Kelso was in too much pain to make fun of the goofy couple. He wished they were at the hospital and he was in less pain.

Kelso and Tom drove down the drive and turned onto the road just as Penny surfaced in the threshold of the doorway. She was crying but trying not to as she waved goodbye. She didn't even get to kiss Kelso goodbye. She really wanted to be in that car.

All of sudden, a wave of anger came over her, and she resented having to take care of her sister's son. What was Nance thinking leaving Samuel with them? *What do we know about kids?* Penny thought to herself. She should be at the hospital with her husband. She texted Nance that now was not a good time to be dropping off Samuel after all. Nance texted back that it was too bad and that they were on their way. She would see them in a few hours.

Penny became even more irritated. It was a good thing she had Jasmine around to take her mind off of things. She was glad she could talk to Jasmine about anything. Jasmine asked Penny if they could pray. Penny had her cross in her pocket of her jogging shorts and decided to put it around her neck.

The word heretic came to mind. Penny knew it was weird and even perhaps wrong. She was Jewish, and technically the Messiah had not come to rescue and save the Israeli nation as of yet. Despite her knowledge she was not sure what she believed. Only that any rabbi would not approve of the cross she held. Cross aside prayers were okay. She was excited to pray and felt no guilt in praying.

"Dearest Lord, please protect and guide both Tom and Kelso on their way to the hospital. Please heal Kelso before he even gets to the hospital if it is Your will. Amen," said Jasmine.

"Amen." Penny opened her eyes and looked at Jasmine. "God would do that?" she asked. "God would heal someone just because they asked for it. You would have to be a good person, of course. Kelso is that. He is very good." Tears formed once again in her eyes.

Jasmine grabbed Penny's hand with both of hers and leaned forward. "He's a friend to the sinner and the 'good person' alike. He is a friend to all of us, whether we're good or rotten. Personally, I fall into both categories," Jasmine said and smiled.

"Does your Bible say that? Does the Torah say that?" asked Penny.

Jasmine reached for her phone. "It's New Testament. I'm not sure of the verse. Actually, I have it on my phone." Jasmine asked if Penny would like to hear it.

"It's 1 John 2:1–2. 'And if any man sin, we have an advocate with the Father, Jesus Christ the righteous.'" Jasmine stopped reading. "God loves us all," she said simply.

"Is that the whole verse? Does it say anything about healing?" Penny asked.

Jasmine looked down then read some more. "'My little children, these things write I unto you, that ye sin not. And if any man sin, we have an advocate with the Father, Jesus Christ the righteous: And he is the propitiation for our sins: and not for ours only, but also for the sins of the whole world.'

"As far as healing, God worked many miracles that are documented in the Torah and the New Testament. I would say the majority of the people who were healed in His power were written about in the New Testament. But there were Moses and Elijah, who God worked through to glorify Himself and the Messiah yet to come.

Penny rolled her eyes. "That verse was totally New Testament, but I believe God will heal Kelso."

Jasmine laughed. She asked Penny if she wouldn't mind being left alone for a half an hour while she went for a short run with Silver before they had to pick up Samuel at the airstrip.

"I haven't changed into my street clothes. Can I go with you? I'm not tired, and I usually run twice as far as I did today," said Penny. It almost sounded as if she was begging.

Jasmine noticed that Penny didn't react well to stress and had become a little clingy. She was really looking forward to her run alone, but due to current conditions, it was probably better if she had another running buddy besides Silver.

Jasmine started to open the front door. "What do you think about trying Silver without a leash. I took him to a dog park once or twice, and he was good and stayed closed beside me."

Penny nodded as they let Silver run out the front door. Jasmine shoved the leash into her jacket pocket.

# Chapter 3

# The Hospital

Tom and Kelso pulled up to the small hospital. "If this hospital is less crowded than the other hospital, then I would hate to see that other hospital. Good thing it's still a bit early," said Tom. "Do you know why hospitals are not always so crowded? Take now out of consideration." Tom paused for the punch line. "Because people are not quite dying to come in," he said.

Kelso corrected him and told him that it was cemeteries, not hospitals, that made the joke funny. Tom knew that, but he needed to keep Kelso lucid, and in general Tom was bad with jokes. He felt like most jokes were worth a shot.

Tom slowed the car to a halt. He now had his arm laid on top of his car seat. He directed his attention toward Kelso and put his hand firmly on Kelso's shoulder. "Are you OK with me dropping you off in front with the emergency vehicles? I will be right behind you as soon as I find a parking space," Tom asked but quickly added, "Never mind," as he put his car into drive and swung his vehicle in front of an ambulance. He turned off his car and walked around to the passenger side to help his friend out of the car.

"Hey, you can't park there. You'll have to park

someplace else," said one of two policemen fast approaching.

A security guard who was attending some other people turned around and started to move toward Tom and Kelso. Others who were waiting to go through the hospital double door nearby started to get angry. Others saw it as a possible shortcut into the hospital. It was as if the crowd was about to swarm and storm the entrance.

Arnie, one of the paramedics who worked on the ambulances, was watching as Tom got out of the car and grabbed Kelso from the passenger's side of the automobile. Arnie felt like he had to act quickly as he often was called to do in his line of work.

Arnie was naturally friendly and had been talking to an ER doctor when he stepped in. Most of the paramedics may not have stepped in, but Arnie was different. He was referred to as the Good Samaritan at this hospital, ever since someone from his neighborhood had leaked his nickname, "Sam," which did stand for Good Samaritan. He'd earned this nickname in local communities for his charitable contributions and his readiness to volunteer as a paramedic or fireman.

He now watched as the men came near Tom and Kelso. He had just dropped a patient off in the emergency entrance a few yards away from the double doors and was finishing up his conversation with one of the attending doctors. Arnie rushed over and claimed Kelso as one of his own. The ER doctor just smiled as he held his arm out as to say, "Welcome.'

Kelso put his arm around Arnie's neck and pressed into him as they walked toward the hospital doors.

Arnie turned to Tom. "I'll meet you in the triage unit right inside to the left, through the double doors. Let the security guard know that your friend has already been admitted. Tell them Arnie sent you. Someone should recognize my name," Arnie said.

Tom looked to Kelso for approval. Kelso gave him a nod.

As Tom got back into his car, he noticed a couple of people on the lawn trying to separate out who would need immediate medical attention and be admitted and who would have to continue to wait outside to be let into the hospital. What a madhouse, Tom thought to himself. He started the car and drove to find the nearest parking spot.

He knew it would probably be a hike back to the hospital, as he figured the nearest spot to park would be a couple streets over in front of someone's house. Normally, he would have headed toward the hospital parking. But he'd noticed on the way in that part of the parking garage had been blocked off due to new hospital construction, and the other part had a red digital sign on the other side showing it was full. He hoped he would not have to park more than a mile or two away. He didn't feel comfortable around people anymore. He hoped Kelso wouldn't have to wait alone too long to be seen by Dr. Edge.

In front of the large hospital desk, Kelso stood with Arnie but was still leaning into him with his arm around his neck. Kelso half-heartedly tried to convince Arnie to leave, and he would have to find a seat. Kelso tried to make it clear that he would be fine waiting for whoever was assigned as a practitioner for triage. He also told him that he had a doctor, Dr. Edge, and that he was to meet him at the hospital.

Arnie ignored Kelso's request for him to leave.

Kelso felt light-headed and was glad for Arnie's support, physically. Arnie must have felt it because he insisted that he would stay and wait for Tom to park his car. Kelso watched for Tom but didn't see him. He looked around the waiting room and noticed it was incredibly crowded, and people were acting peculiar—not just injured but ill. There was moaning and groaning coming from various directions of the waiting room. Kelso had thought that there would be more people who were hurt than ill, but he quickly came up with a ratio of about three to one. It seemed like at least 30 percent looked sickly or under the weather.

Arnie also perceived the difference and was uneasy. Arnie told the nurse at the desk, Nurse Bratchet, that he personally would take Kelso back to the critical care unit. "Kelso has already been triaged by me," said the paramedic. He had determined that Kelso was ill; he just hadn't filled out the paperwork.

Nurse Bratchet had just seen Arnie come and go with a patient. She guessed that Kelso was either a friend or someone he was just trying to help out, unless he was Superman and was able to fly. Nurse Bratchet kept a close eye on her virtual manifest of the paramedics and patients being transported. She felt it was part of her job to keep track of the numbers, although it wasn't.

Most of the time, patients who came through the ER entrance of the hospital to be admitted would not even pass by her part of the building, and she would never see them. But Nurse Bratchet still felt connected to every patient, as eventually that patient would show up in her system.

Nurse Bratchet had a very hard time ignoring the scantily filled out patient information by Arnie. "You have to fill out your normal paperwork, too," she reminded Arnie, with her raised eyebrows raised.

Arnie knew that he would be in deep trouble if the paperwork ever caught up with him, but he barely thought twice about it. He looked at his watch and wondered what was keeping Tom.

Tom made it to the front of the hospital and explained his situation to the security guard. Although many people had objected to Tom pushing to the front of the line, Tom was let though the hospital doors.

He quickly found Nurse Bratchet's desk and joined them as Arnie filled out the last of Kelso's paperwork. "I filled out his insurance information and some other of his history, although Kelso may not have been paying close attention to the questions I was asking. Is he allergic to any medications?" Arnie asked.

Kelso shook his head.

Tom answered no for Kelso.

Arnie started on his own paperwork. Kelso was now hunched over, sitting behind Arnie in one of the waiting room chairs. He asked Kelso some triage questions. Nurse Bratchet handed Tom's ID and insurance card to Arnie, who handed it to Tom, who handed it to Kelso. Kelso looked up; a ghostly pale face emerged, which caught both Arnie and Tom off guard. Kelso slid the cards back into his wallet. Arnie reached over and felt his lymph nodes as he continued to ask Kelso about his symptoms.

Nurse Bratchet looked up and asked for his almost completed documents. She asked him about the diagnosis and looked down at the paperwork. She told him that this would do it, and he could be on his way.

Arnie knew she was doing him a huge solid. "He most likely has ruptured his spleen or soon will. He is dehydrated and likely has mononucleosis, depending on what the blood work turns up."

As he was talking to Nurse Bratchet, a man who had earlier seemed to be growling at him, stood up and took a couple of steps toward Arnie and then, as if someone had thrown cold water on him, the man fell back down in his seat.

"That was weird," Nurse Bratchet exclaimed.

The nurse had slid one more piece of paper in front of Arnie to sign and to have Kelso sign. She also handed to Tom his guest badge and some hospital information to give to Kelso. Everything had been entered into the system, and Kelso was ready to be escorted.

But once again, the man making strange noises stood up. This time, he made a tenor-sounding grunt noise and came at Arnie. Arnie's hand started to shake, but he didn't turn around as he finished his signature. Nurse Bratchet let out a yelp that sounded more like a small Pekinese dog bark. She looked around for help. An officer made eye contact with her and quickly made his way over to her desk.

Officer Goodman was on duty at the nurses' station. He had been assigned to crowd control. He reacted quickly, coming at the grunting man and telling him he needed to wait until he was called into triage. The man growled and mumbled something incoherent at the officer.

"Did he just growl at me?" The officer looked innocently at the nurse and Arnie, while standing between the man and Arnie. "You had better sit down," said the officer and put his hand on his club.

Kelso who hated violence, faked losing his balance while standing up and strategically fell into the troublemaker. The man lost all coordination and flopped back into his chair. His head twisted back. He then flipped sideward as if he was going to sleep and closed his eyes.

"That was weird," Kelso said, repeating Nurse Bratchet's words.

The officer said to the nurse, "You should probably see this guy next," and pointed to the guy flopped over in his chair, whose eyes were still closed.

Nurse Bratchet agreed and picked up the phone. She said a few words. And before she'd hung up, a triage attendant came at warp speed and checked the man's pulse.

He—the man passed out on the chair, Mr. Unger— had already filled out the necessary paperwork when he'd come in. She picked up his paperwork once again to see if there was a hint of his condition but was surprised that everything appeared to be neatly handwritten and in order. Nurse Bratchet then, as always, watched closely to make sure that Mr. Unger was admitted quickly.

Arnie waited for Nurse Bratchet's attention and pointed to the double doors. She gave him the go-ahead and, in turn, hit a button on her desk that turned the red light above the door to a green light. The guard that stood beside the door looked up at the green light and moved further to the right to let Arnie, Kelso, and Tom pass as the automatic doors opened.

Kelso was sandwiched between Arnie and Tom as they walked him back into the intensive care unit. The ICU was usually quiet. But tonight, it was humming with activity. The hospital staff was trying to accommodate patients with a limited facility. There was some construction work being done in different parts of the hospital. Much of the hospital had been damaged by the recent earthquake, including the critical care unit that joined the intensive care unit.

Kelso already knew that much of the hospital's overflow had been handled by transferring patients to the main hospital in Los Angeles per his conversation with Dr. Edge. He knew he was lucky to be seen so swiftly at this hospital and could not imagine what it would be like if some of the hospital's patients were not transported. He wasn't sure if even Dr. Edge would have been able to get him in so quickly.

Nurse Kinder met with Arnie immediately. Another nurse grabbed a wheelchair and pushed it toward Arnie and walked away. Arnie caught the wheelchair and thanked the nurse. Arnie and Tom helped Kelso into the wheelchair.

Nurse Kinder was pleased to see Arnie. It was obvious to Tom and Kelso that she was smitten with Arnie's curly, blond locks; serious, dark blue eyes; and tall, muscular build as she swept herself next to him, rubbing her arm against his. "Arnie, it's an awful night for me to do you any favors. Nurse Bratchet already briefed me via text. Texts can be a lifesaver, but enough chit chat. I have a room, B384; it's on the third floor, at the end of the hall." Like Nurse Bratchet, she had also assumed that Kelso was a friend of Arnie's. Why would he go out of his way for someone he didn't know? she thought to herself. "For now he will be the only person in that room. It was being saved for someone, but I can make a mistake or two and get away with it, just like you." Nurse Kinder smiled at Arnie, hoping he would notice her big, beautiful blue eyes. "It's the best I can do. I can't guarantee that he'll be seen by a doctor anytime soon. Is he a friend or just a stray? Nurse Bratchet wanted to know."

"A bit unprofessional, but he is a friend. So take good care of him," said Arnie.

Kelso and Tom exchanged looks. Tom patted Arnie on the back in agreement.

It was then that Dr. Edge walked into the unit. "I can take it from here. Sorry I'm late, Kelso. I parked in the garage but had to walk around the building to come in the front due to hospital construction." Dr. Edge turned to the paramedic. "You must be Arnie. I checked in at the front lobby to see if Kelso had made it in yet and met with Nurse Bratchet. She said you would be back here. She also mentioned that, if it weren't for a certain paramedic, he would still be out there waiting—or worse, on the front lawn waiting to be let in. Thank you for getting Kelso in so quickly. I am sure you are extremely busy and there are a few more runs you have to make today."

"You're right; it has been nonstop." Arnie said and turned to around to say goodbye. "Godspeed, Kelso. It was a pleasure meeting you, Tom. Stay safe," said Arnie.

Arnie leaned down and whispered something in Kelso's ear. Tom was able to hear part of the whisper as well. Tom heard something about staying or being safe. Kelso looked at him oddly and told him thanks for everything. "It's the second time someone said Godspeed to me today."

Arnie suggested to Kelso that the origin of *Godspeed* was worth looking up. Tom reached out and firmly shook Arnie's hand and thanked him.

As Arnie was leaving Dr. Edge started to complain about paramedics. "Sometimes I think paramedics just don't know how to make the most of their time. Most people think of them as heroes, always coming to the rescue, but efficiency is everything."

He would have continued but Nurse Kinder interrupted. She had a printed schedule that she held in her hand. "Arnie acted very bravely. He works twice as hard as any doctor I know, but with less pay," she said. Her cheeks were flushed.

Dr. Edge pretended not to hear her.

"Dr. Edge, I don't have you on the schedule. In fact, I don't have you on the schedule for the next two weeks. Are you here to volunteer? It still should be on the schedule—unless you didn't tell anyone you were coming. Are you supposed to volunteer at this hospital or Central, because Central may need you more than we do, although we really could use you here?" Nurse Kinder was a person who processed her thoughts out loud, by talking. She looked at the doctor, perplexed. "Volunteer here, please Dr. Edge. We really need you," she added, now pleading with the doctor.

Kelso, Tom, and Dr. Edge felt the desperation in her voice.

Dr. Edge quietly stood for what seemed to be a minute. "I was supposed to be on PTO for the next two weeks, Honduras, but I had to cancel my plans. I'll try to make myself useful wherever I can, dear," said Dr. Edge. She pulled him aside and continued to talk with him.

Tom's inquisitive nature got the best of him. "Does your doctor do mission work in Honduras?" asked Tom. "Does he belong to a church? Has he done mission work in any other countries? We have friends who are part of Doctors Without Borders; he may have crossed paths with them."

The expression was disgust. "How the hell should I know what church he belongs to or who he works with when he vacations? He's only my doctor. We don't hang out and have beers," answered Kelso now visibly in pain.

Dr. Edge came back over to Kelso in his wheelchair and Tom standing behind it. "We had better get him to his room quickly. Kelso, we'll get you some good medication and have you feeling better in no time. Nurse, what was that room number again?" asked Dr. Edge.

Nurse Kinder repeated the number.

Tom, Kelso, and Dr. Edge slid inside the medical elevator and headed to the third floor.

# Chapter 4

## *The Airstrip*

*J*asmine and Penny started down the driveway at a good pace. They went along the same route that Penny and Kelso had traveled that morning except for that they had doubled back eastward; Jasmine and Penny headed only west down their street. They were laughing as Penny related the story of the two robbers. "The would-be thieves said, if it weren't for the dog, we probably would have been victims of a robbery."

Penny stopped laughing. They both looked around for Silver. Jasmine stopped and patted Silver, who had been running a close clip behind them.

Penny was excited to be running with Silver for the first time. "He will make you a good running partner. I am excited for you," said Jasmine.

Penny had already thought of that. "You're much more of a dog person than I am. Are you sure you don't want to take Silver back home after all this chaos settles?" she asked.

Jasmine shook her head as she pointed ahead. She and Penny slowed to a halt. Several people had just turned onto their street from a side road and were walking haphazardly toward them. "Penny, look. Who are they? That doesn't look good, especially after the story you told me about looters being this far out." Jasmine pulled the leash from her jacket pocket and hooked onto Silver's collar.

Silver panted and wagged his tail as they slowed to a stop and his leash was attached. Jasmine was grateful that the stranglers were far enough away that Silver didn't bark or growl. They were unnoticed for now.

Penny's face went white. "They don't look normal. They look ill," said Penny. "They look like the undead, bedraggled and disheveled. They have a similar appearance to Kelso this morning." They crouched along the side of the road. They hoped that they would not be seen as they made their way home.

"Follow me." Penny led Jasmine and Silver up the hill to the running path that led back to their house.

They walked a little bit down the path and again let Silver off his leash. They sprinted back to the house. Silver kept up behind them. Penny burst through the door first. Jasmine was a close second.

"Pancakes and then a shower? Do you think we should be worried?" asked Penny as she drew large breaths of air.

Jasmine nodded in agreement with the idea of pancakes and a shower, although she would have preferred the opposite order of things. She waited a minute until she could answer Penny's second question without having to breath in too heavily.

"Maybe. Did you recognize any of those people? We may have overreacted, but they did seem out of sorts. I don't think they had a chance to see us. They certainly couldn't have followed us back, especially you. Do you always run that fast at the end of a run?"

"No and no. On occasion, I do. As for recognizing anyone, I didn't. It's not unusual for me not to know our neighbors; I'm somewhat of a recluse. I'm not that neighborly. Also, our neighbors are a little spread out here, so we don't see them on a regular basis. But I am familiar with their names. I even know what they paid for their houses and when they bought them. I just don't know how much they owe," said Penny. She blushed as she realized that she may have come across as a busybody. "We got a pretty good deal on our house," said Penny.

Both Penny and Jasmine laughed.

Penny and Jasmine waited until 10:30 a.m. to leave for the airstrip. They piled a few things and themselves into True Blue. Silver road in the back as he had before when Penny had brought him home.

True Blue was driven up the dusty and partly paved road to the nearly abandoned airstrip. There, they waited for Nancy and Samuel's plane to land. The plane was late.

They looked around for anything out of the ordinary at the airstrip. But everything looked normal for an airstrip that had little use. Jasmine took something out of her purse and laid it on the ground. It rolled like a ball and then intermittently stopped. She ran after it and picked it up again. She then pulled out her phone and entered in some numbers. "There, that should do it," she said. She set the ball back on the ground, and it went sailing.

"I am not asking," Penny said but was too curious. "How do you keep it in perpetual motion? It is just an electronic ball. It doesn't shoot lasers?" Penny thought about the tricked-out phone Jasmine had wanted her to take a couple of days ago. Kelso had said that the phone was not tricked out, but Tom and Jasmine were just well versed at technology and that she was not, but Penny knew better. "How about the stop and start? How does that work? It cannot be totally round."

Silver wanted to chase the miniature bowling ball. Penny held tightly to his leash.

The ball zagged and then took off. "Not just a ball but a camera. And it is round. It has a motor on the inside. It has gears and weights that keep it going and is controllable virtually by my smartphone. I have it set so that it can navigate its own perimeters, the perimeters I set on my phone. It's like a landlocked drone but less conspicuous and does not have to be registered with the FAA. It will automatically stop when its motion detectors sense anyone within a few kilometers and start to roll back. It's like it's on autopilot. I have it set to take a few pictures every fifteen meters up to two kilometers and then come directly back." Jasmine explained. She quickly looked at the images that were streamed to her phone.

Penny pulled a real tennis ball out of her jacket pocket after letting Silver off his leash. "It can be a few miles away before returning home if you program it to do so?", asked Penny. Jasmine nodded.

Silver was quick to bring the tennis ball back to Penny. Jasmine examined her pictures. There were enough pictures to have a preliminary view of the airfield. She picked up the camera ball and placed it in her bag. She joined Penny in taking turns tossing the tennis ball to Silver.

Penny and Jasmine played ball with Silver as they waited and talked about nonsensical things. Penny talked about why there were different type of clouds and how so many things of nature served specific purposes that build onto each other. Jasmine agreed and added that the ecosystem in general was a hierarchy of purpose, and it seemed to her that there was an imbalance to everything that was occurring in the world as of recent. She was inclined to believe that one event was setting off the next like a domino effect. Penny didn't ask her to explain. Penny was just glad that, for now, the craziness of life was lost in the peace of tossing the ball to each other and Silver.

Penny's pocket vibrated, and reality returned. Kelso's text read that he would be at the hospital for at least a couple of days. And she was right; it was mononucleosis. Dr. Edge had done his blood work, and his spleen had almost ruptured. He also had a bacterial infection that Dr. Edge was treating with an antibiotic. He was already feeling better.

Penny saw the text and quickly replied, "OK." She put her phone back in her pocket. She then received another message—this time from her sister, who said her plane would be a few hours late. She was glad she had packed a small cooler with lunch for Jasmine and herself. She had also packed snacks and a sandwich for Samuel in case he got hungry, although their house wasn't far from the airstrip.

Penny told Jasmine about the delay of the plane and that Kelso would not be home for a few days. Jasmine asked a couple of questions about Kelso and Tom, which

Penny could not answer, so Jasmine decided to let it go. Instead of heading back home, they decided to make an afternoon of it. They selected a spot to have a picnic lunch at the airfield but would wait a little while before they ate. Penny picked up the ball and continued to play toss with Jasmine and Silver.

Penny promised herself that she would not resent Sam for having to be left in her care. She loved her sister and her family, but she yearned to be with Kelso. Every fiber of her being told her that she had everything to lose, but she had to push those thoughts aside and pull it together for her family. Even more than she wished for her and Kelso's well-being, she wished for faith that would encompass all her thoughts and circumstances. But the times required action, not sentiment. She swallowed hard as she felt her eyes start to water.

Finally, Jasmine and Penny could see a small dot in the sky. Penny pulled out a small pair of binoculars that Jasmine and Penny shared. As it drew near, they were sure it was the company's private plane. As it drew even closer, they could see a little individual in particular waving as the plane lowered its landing gear and came to a stop.

As the door of the plane opened, a slightly hesitant but anxious boy appeared. Samuel was grinning from ear to ear. He was as excited to be there as Penny was happy to see him. Penny would love Samuel as her own, but it was a difficult time for her and Kelso.

Nancy deliberately took her time getting off the plane. She cautiously watched the steps down. From the distance, Penny noticed that her sister stepped down like she was hurt. Then Penny remembered that Nancy had injured herself going down the stairs and was in therapy. She had injured her hip but had told Penny it was better.

Sam had already made his way over to Penny and hugged her around the waist. She smiled down at him. "How's my favorite nephew?" said Penny.

Samuel looked up with his arms still around her waist and said, "Your only nephew."

Penny was glad Sam was a clever boy.

"Mom says that she should have a nephew or niece too and that it's unfair that she doesn't," said Sam. He waited for his aunt's reaction but there was none. She just smiled.

"This will be an adventure. And when your mother is done with her work, then you will have another exciting life experience. You'll go stay with Grandma and Grandpa at the mountain house. You can do all the fun things that we use to do, but with Grandma and Grandpa. You can swing on the swings, play games, go hiking or fishing. And I bet you still love to swim. So you will have a double adventure this year," said Penny.

Penny had a habit of being very direct. Kelso had warned her to stay away from elaborating on any possible side effects of the "cons" of his situation or the "cons" themselves. Her words were to instill an aspect of fun and shy him away from the severity of current events. Whether it worked or not, she could only hope.

"It's OK, Auntie; even if we do boring things together, I know it will be fun. It doesn't have to be an adventure, and I would rather be with you and Uncle Kelso then with Grandma and Grandpa. I see them a lot, but I don't get to see you that often," Sam said.

Penny missed Sam. All the memories of babysitting,

teaching him how to read, playing board games, and just hanging out together at the family unions came flooding back to her frontal lobe. He helped her to not focus just on herself. Sam brought a different vantage point. Sam's outlook was one of simplicity, faith, and love—a child's perspective.

"Where's Uncle Kelso?" asked Sam. He looked so much older than he had the last time she'd seen him. "He said he would teach me how to catch if I hadn't already learned how," said Samuel.

"You don't know how to catch a ball?" Penny asked teasingly, but she knew what he meant.

"No. I can catch a regular baseball but not grounders and fly balls. It's complicated, but does that make sense?" Sam asked as he tilted his head as if he had just said something very profound.

Penny could see her sister tilting her head and asking Samuel a question in the same manner. She eagerly agreed with him that it made all the sense in the world.

Nance walked over and gave Penny a firm one-armed hug and dropped Sam's bags beside her. "Thanks, sis,' she said. 'This means everything to me. I would not be able to do my job if Samuel was not with you and Kelso. I owe you."

Penny put her hand on Samuel's head and said it was not a problem. This time she did not hesitate to say so because she meant it. It was not an inconvenience, but a blessing Penny told herself. "I am thankful for you letting me have him for a little while. I'm sure we'll have lots of fun. By the way, this is my friend Jasmine. She and her husband are staying with us for a little while," Penny added.

Jasmine curtsied before Nancy and Sam. Nancy held out her hand. And Jasmine, who was a little embarrassed, held out hers; the two of them shook hands. Jasmine then turned to Sam, who put one of his arms behind his back and one in front of his stomach and bowed and giggled, which made Jasmine laugh.

"Listen, Penny, I don't have a lot of time to talk. So put your listening ears on. There is a state of war that may be declared against Iran. We're sure that the Iranian government is trying to take advantage of some of the situations happening around the world, especially in neighboring countries. Hostile actions are also being aimed at Israel and the United States." Nancy paused to take in her surroundings.

Jasmine stared into the distance but was soaking up every word.

"Now this part affects you directly," Nancy continued, making sure she had Penny's undivided attention. "There's an epidemic outbreak that may be flulike but more serious. They, some of the best scientists, cannot even narrow it down to exactly which type of virus strain it is or, less specific, to which flu is most similar—in other words, pig, bird, or something else. But it has all of us concerned. It's definitely more serious than just the flu, although I don't know the death count. Some speculate that it's not a virus at all but bacterial, which may actually be worse if you look at some of the ramifications of how it could be spreading so quickly." Again, Nancy paused and saw the concern on Penny's face.

"Sweetheart, I am not telling you this to worry you but so you, Kelso, and your friends can take precautions.

You know what do to in this type of situation. Stay away from hospitals. Drink only bottled water. Keep your hands clean. And if you come into contact with individuals with pale skin, bloodshot eyes, and listless behavior, go the other way. Do not try to help them. I will text you other indicators of an infected person, but I, in general, would suggest you stay away from people. Especially, keep Samuel out of any precarious situation. Where's Kelso?" asked Nancy.

"Kelso is at the hospital," Penny said.

Nancy's eyes got big. She looked at Samuel and then back at Jasmine. "Well, that is a problem," said Nancy. "Can you tell me what his symptoms are and what happened?"

Penny showed Nancy the text Kelso had sent her.

"This may be big, little sis, so tell him to stay away from other people and to keep his hands clean. Tell him to wash them, not just use sanitizer. Did he go to the hospital alone?" Nancy asked.

"No, my husband, Tom, went with him. I 've already texted him your instructions. Thank you for that," said Jasmine.

Nancy could come to a quick estimation of a person's character within sixty seconds and be right. She looked at Jasmine and immediately knew with whom she was talking, not an equal of intellect but a contender and someone of status. Nancy could see that Jasmine was a person of discipline and efficiency.

"Jasmine, it will be fine if Sam stays with you if Penny has to go be with Kelso for a day or two." She looked at Penny and smiled as to say I love my sister but not all the choices she makes. "But at no time and in no way is Samuel to go near any hospitals, especially since there is a real possibility of lockdowns at some of the hospitals. Sorry for leaving that part out, but much of our intelligence is on a need-to-know basis," said Nancy.

Jasmine stared blankly. She could not believe the difference in personalities between Nancy and her sister. Penny's face was pale as a ghost.

Jasmine thought to say something, but Nancy just continued to talk in short sentences. She too could estimate people and knew anything she had to say was not important enough for Nancy to pause and regard. Jasmine also did not want to get on a person of intelligence's bad side or ask too many questions and risk that she herself might be called into question. She remained quiet.

"Don't worry, Penny. Kelso and you will be fine. I am to meet with the chief of staff and perhaps the secretary of state as soon as we land in DC. Then after we brief, we could meet with the president. I will check in with you soon after that. You're holding up, right?", she took her sister by her shoulders and put her face up to Penny's face and looked intensely into her sister's eyes.

"Nancy, everything will be fine. Go save the world or at least our little corner. I will stay here with Samuel and wait for Kelso to come home," said Penny.

"That's the spirit," Nancy said in an attaboy tone. "Gotta go." She leaned in and put her cheek next to Penny's as she embraced her. She then crouched down and pulled Samuel close to her. "Were you paying attention to everything I was saying?" Nancy asked rhetorically.

"Mother, I don't want to stay with Jasmine. If my Aunt

Penny goes to be with Uncle Kelso, I want to go too. I don't know her. She is not part of our family," said Sam.

Nancy blushed. "Sam, this is serious." Nancy paused to give Samuel a moment to focus. "What is it that I am asking of you?" she asked.

"You want me to trust, listen, and obey," said Samuel.

"And?" She looked at her son as her eyes widened.

"You want me to be aware of my surrounding at all times. I have a cell phone that I am to keep charged every day and an extra battery in my pocket in case it isn't charged. Did you also know the extra battery has a cool flashlight?" Samuel said as his eyes widened. His mom just smiled. "Mom, I am going to miss you." Sam threw his arms around his mother's neck. Samuel tried hard not to cry, but his eyes were watering.

Samuel and Nancy had been through many conversations as to why he could not stay by his mother's side—how, even if he was quiet at all times, he still couldn't come with her. He knew what she was doing was very important, and there was no one else for this job. He consoled himself only in the fact it was not her job to disarm nuclear bombs. He thought to himself then there would be problems.

"I love you, champ," said Nancy. "I will keep in touch and see you soon. Remember, we can video chat through the phone but not too much."

Samuel nodded.

There was a man now standing by the stairs to the plane. He looked like a government agent with his dark sunglasses and dark suit. "Jasmine, it was nice meeting you. Thank you for your help. Penny, keep it together.

This is the stuff for which you are made. Thank you both for your assistance." She gave Jasmine a quick glance, telling her to take care of Penny for her.

Jasmine's smiled and thought to herself, *This is not the stuff for which Penny is made.* That was unless Nancy was talking about motherhood — a blessing she prayed for for both Penny and herself.

They watched as Nancy boarded the plane— except for Samuel, who had accepted his situation. He held his Aunt Penny's hand and gazed at his auntie's face. He wanted to keep her there for as long as he could. It was the first time that Jasmine really wished Tom was there with her to help make sense of everything.

"OK, Samuel, let's get going. Are you hungry?" Penny asked as they headed back to the car.

The plane taxied down the small runway.

"Not really," he said as he turned his head to take one last look at the plane. The wheels lifted off of the ground, and his mother took off for her new destination. *I am not going to be sad*, he thought to himself. *This is an adventure*, he repeated.

Jasmine, Penny, and Samuel climbed into True Blue and headed home. It would take about twenty minutes before they would turn onto their street. Samuel took out his headsets and plugged it into his phone.

# Chapter 5

# When Can We Get Out of This Place?

Kelso drifted off in his hospital bed, glad the medication was taking over. He knew he needed to rest. While he was sleeping, Tom was getting an inordinate number of texts from Jasmine. She promised she would call or text him as soon as they got home, and Penny and Samuel got settled.

Tom wanted to wake Kelso but also knew he needed rest and sleep. Apparently, the bacterial infection for which he was treated could be pretty serious and infectious. Dr. Edge had said he was glad it hadn't entered the bloodstream but hadn't said much more about the origin or nature of the infection. At that time, Tom hadn't been sure what questions to ask Dr. Edge. Now as Kelso lay there, he thought of several things he wanted to know about Kelso and his illnesses.

Tom stuck his head out of the door to see what was going on in the hospital. He was glad nothing was happening, especially in their hallway. It was quiet on their floor—to the extent it was eerie. It was like the last night that they'd spent in their condo. The streets beneath them were vacant and without the normal excitement of living downtown. It just was not a normal quiet.

Dr. Edge allowed Tom to stay in Kelso's room, since Kelso's mononucleosis contagion was limited, but the doctor wouldn't let any other patient share a room with Kelso. Dr. Edge asked Tom to make sure Kelso had no visitors. He was not only concerned about the spreading of mononucleosis but about the bacterial infection Kelso had contracted.

Kelso had developed hives on his chest and also on his back on his way to the hospital. He hadn't discovered them until he'd been examined by Dr. Edge. It was after his run that Kelso had first started to feel itchy. The doctor couldn't tell Kelso exactly what the hives were from but was sure the bacterial infection, irritated spleen, and extra exertion of physical activity had something to do with it. The doctor had immediately treated the hives with prednisone and an antihistamine.

Tom sat in his chair eating an energy bar and contemplating what he would tell Kelso when he woke. The information Jasmine had sent him via email, besides the texts she'd add also sent, was abundant. That, coupled with other information from Twitter and Facebook, was overwhelming. It was information that was incomplete. He was still piecemealing together. Any answer he had led to more questions.

Tom pondered the strange behavior of the man who was waiting to be triaged and Arnie's whisper. Arnie had whispered a warning to keep safe and alert and stay away from people in this hospital. As a medic, Arnie was known to hospital staff and other people as someone who cares and is there for people in the most difficult situations. He was not only resourceful, but relentless for achieving the best results. He must have seen and experienced some interesting events, Tom thought to himself.

Tom respected Arnie but could not account for the warning or his fear. Why had Arnie's hands been shaking as he'd signed Kelso in? It was almost like Arnie knew how sick the man was who'd approached him from behind at the nurse's desk—the man the nurse had noted would be admitted immediately. Arnie just held fast to the task at hand despite his fearfulness. He truly was a nice guy.

Tom thought about keeping most of what he knew from Kelso, but then he decided against it. Intelligent people could do a lot of good with more information as long as they can maintain perspective. What would be the use, anyway? Facts had a way of being revealed. Kelso would find out eventually. Kelso's phone started vibrating with a text from Penny. It a was a message letting him know she couldn't talk or text with him directly until they were safe at home. She had inadvertently left her Bluetooth headset at home charging in its adapter.

Jasmine was text chatting with four different people. She was affectively texting for Penny since she was driving. Jasmine had Penny's phone and was forwarding the information that Nancy had emailed and texted to Penny to her own phone so she would also have a copy. Tom told Jasmine to stop texting Kelso; he was in need of rest.

Tom also didn't want Kelso to feel the pressure of having to answer the texts when he woke up. Jasmine realized she would not be seeing Tom tonight. Tom had taken the position of nanny. Jasmine had asked about the hives, since that was on Nancy's list of symptoms. Tom peaked down Kelso's shirt to see if they were still there.

"What the hell are you doing?" asked Kelso as he reached up and grabbed Tom's arm. "And why is my phone going off every two seconds and your phone too?" He tried to sit up in bed but found it difficult. "Is Penny all right? Hey, listen. Even if I'm sleeping or really drugged up, let me know if anything has happened. Penny is OK, right?"

Tom looked at Kelso, wondering what he should tell him and what he shouldn't. "Penny is OK," said Tom.

"Why is our hospital room door shut?" asked Kelso.

Tom just looked at the door. "Do you want me to open it?" he asked.

"Yeah, I would like to see who's coming and going. I'm going to try to stay awake for a while now so you can catch me up. I think Prednisone makes me jumpy anyway," Kelso replied.

Tom opened the door. He immediately heard the nurses arguing about something trivial, and he felt a little bit better. Tom was getting freaked out by all of Jasmine's texts. He couldn't believe that they may be in the middle of an epidemic on top of everything else that was going on in California and all over the world. He looked back at Kelso when he'd opened the door halfway.

"Open it all the way."

Tom obeyed and came and then sat down in a chair next to Kelso's bed.

Kelso had looked at his chest and showed Tom. It

was a little difficult, since he wasn't used to having an IV hooked up to him. The doctor had been trying to hydrate him quickly, as well as drip barbiturates into his system. "See. The hives are almost gone. I probably just need some antibiotics and some rest. Tom, you look frazzled."

Tom was responding to Jasmine's text, letting her that the hives were better. Tom's phone continued to vibrate. Kelso's phone had finally stop vibrating.

Kelso positioned his bed to sit himself up. "Spill it. What the hell is going on?" asked Kelso. He looked at his watch. It was 3:00 p.m.

The news was bad. "Just one second. Jasmine, let me call you back? I assume you made it home safely. No, the door is open. I just opened it. I know it's important, but no one is going to just walk into the room and spread some cursed virus. Yes, I read all your texts. The hives are going away. Did you get my last text? The doctor says it was probably due to too much physical activity in combination with this illness. Yes, he's awake."

Kelso's phone started to play the tune "Up, Up and Away, My Beautiful Balloon." Penny and Kelso liked to play pranks on each other, and she had changed Kelso's ringtone.

Tom started to laugh and so did Jasmine, who heard the tune through his phone. It continued until Tom walked across the room and picked up the phone on Kelso's folded pants and shirts. "Would you like to fly in my beautiful, my beautiful balloon?" asked Tom.

Tom handed the phone to Kelso. The ring tone continued to play until Kelso said, "Hi Beautiful."

Penny apologized for the change of ringtones, which she knew at any other time would be funny.

Acting casual came natural to Kelso. "It's still funny. I am not seriously ill, Pen. No worries," said Kelso.

The somber mood on the other side of the phone was flagrant. "So, you are OK?" Penny asked. "I know you have to rest, so I don't plan on staying on the phone for too long. I really miss you, you know. You do know?" asked Penny.

Kelso looked at his phone and brought it back up to his ear. "What do I know? That you were lucky to land such a fine male specimen as myself? Or is that I am in as much love with you as you are with me? Relax, Penny. I'll be home soon. I need a day or so of rest and inactivity, and then I will be fine. Besides, I'm sure I'm in one of the safest places right now. Tom told me the hospital has added extra security."

Dr. Edge walked in while Kelso was talking to Penny. Kelso waved. The doctor checked his vitals. Kelso wondered why the doctor was checking his vitals and not a nurse like before, and then he remembered that he probably was Dr. Edge's only real patient, since he was supposed to be on vacation.

Without warning, a wave a sleepiness fell over him. "Dr. Edge is here. Can I call you back in a while?" Kelso asked.

Penny knew the right thing was to let Kelso just rest this evening, and she could talk with him tomorrow, but she did not want to stop talking to him.

Penny knew Kelso was in good hands with Tom. She had additionally reasoned that he was pretty doped up and wouldn't remember much of what they said. So she could hang up anytime, but she held online for just a little longer before she said what she felt was needed. "I will call you tomorrow. We're safe and sound. I moved the gun to a shelf in the closet since Samuel is staying with us. But it's easy to reach for Jasmine and me. I believe if there are any trespassers, Silver will bark, giving us a proper warning. As for our family and us, my sister arrived safely in DC, and she will be meeting with the secretary of state shortly. Mom and Dad are setting up house in the country with their neighbors the Kurts. Samuel, Jasmine, and I are playing rummy and snacking out on junk food. That about covers it." Penny sounded happy.

Kelso picked up on Penny's happiness. "Junk food? Do we have junk food?" he asked.

Penny laughed. "Popcorn with salt and butter," she said. "I make the best junk food around." Penny looked at Samuel and Jasmine, who both gave her a thumbs-up.

Kelso was not going to be able to stay awake too much longer. He realized he was pretty medicated. "Not sure if popcorn counts as junk food, even with extra butter." He laughed. "I'll talk with you tomorrow. Text me goodnight before you go to bed." He ended the call and turned his attention to Dr. Edge.

Kelso led with his questions. "So, Doc, when do you think we can leave this place and get back home to our families? I am feeling much better and can recover just as well resting at home."

Dr. Edge turned to Kelso. "That's a good question, since I live within the same area as you. Tom could go home now. And when you're ready to be released, I could drive you home. I don't plan on putting in excessive hours, since I'm not the attending physician for anyone except you. I'm still considered on volunteer status. I also want to be free to assist at Central Hospital. There are some interesting cases at Central."

Tom studied the Doctor. The doctor did not know about the epidemic. "No. I'm staying. Hey, do you know anything about an epidemic, doc?" asked Tom.

Kelso did not know what to make of the question.

Dr. Edge looked back down at his tablet and then at Tom. "No, but there have been some questions raised. I will let you know what I hear and try to get you two out of here if that is the case. Are you sure you want to stay?"

Jasmine had already texted Tom about the possibility of a lockdown, but he didn't feel right leaving Kelso. Dr. Edge also seemed to have his best interest at heart. "Nurse Bratchet from downstairs checked in on us during her break," Tom replied. She had a rollaway bed sent to our room so I could sleep here tonight. I'm impressed with the efficiency of the hospital staff here. But, Doc, I'm all set up. It would be a shame to leave now. I imagine they'll even feed me if I ask politely."

Dr. Edge wasn't sure why Tom would want to stay with Kelso. "OK, then. Make sure you order food for yourself when you turn in Kelso's food order with the nurse, or you will not be fed. You will not want to go to the cafeteria. The lines are horrible there. You also could come down with a virus from someone or something from which you came in contact." Dr. Edge he was really issuing a warning. "As for your question as to how long we will be keeping you, I anticipate at least another day. I will try to get you boys out of here as soon as I can. You should be thankful your spleen didn't rupture. With that amount of pain, well, let's just say I am glad—very, very glad—that you came when you did. Did you have any other questions for me?"

Kelso was now closing his eyes as he talked. He had almost lost his train of thought. "Doc, I don't mind the Prednisone and the strong antibiotic, but could you ease up on the pain medication or just eliminate it. I can do without it, I think. I would rather have a clear head," he said.

The doctor looked at his chart again. "How did I miss this? This is not right. This is twice as much as I had prescribed. Ah, there's another doctor's name on your chart, who must have increased it."

Tom, who was already standing, went to the doctor's side and leaned over the doctor's shoulder to look at the chart. He wondered if he'd heard the doctor correctly.

"Yes, we will lower your pain medication tonight and take you off it by tomorrow morning," Dr. Edge said. 'I agree. You need to try to be alert. But for now, get some rest."

Kelso smiled with his eyes closed.

"Tom, did Nurse Bratchet look at this chart?" asked Dr. Edge.

Tom saw immediately where the question was headed. "Yes, she looked at his chart, but she didn't change anything. Should she have? She said something to Kelso about being in a lot of pain, which he was. I don't know who that other doctor is, but he hasn't been in to see Kelso yet," he added.

Dr. Edge looked confused for the first time. "It's definitely enough to keep your friend comfortable. Tom, keep an eye on Kelso. If he needs anything or if anything doesn't seem right, just call me." Dr. Edge took hold of Kelso's arm and removed the needle that was attached to his IV bags. "Actually, we'll be taking him off his pain medication now. He should be fine for sleeping through the night. I am noting it on his chart."

Dr. Edge leaned down to where Tom was now sitting. "Tom", he continued, "if he wakes up and wants pain medication again, talk him out of it and remind him what he agreed to—lower medication and then no medication. By 3:00 a.m., if he wakes up, he won't feel the pain medication but, rather, will start to feel the residual effects of the medication. He might experience dry mouth, diarrhea, numbness, and perhaps a headache."

Dr. Edge paused and pulled his phone out of his pocket. "What's your cell phone number?" he asked.

Tom gave it to him, and the doctor dialed the number. "Now, you have my emergency pager number. Kelso has my regular home and cell number. Don't lose it." Dr. Edge shook Tom's hand. As he exited and was shutting the door, he looked up and said one last thing, "Let's keep this door shut. There have been some people wandering the halls. Luckily, your hall is undisturbed."

Tom did not like the serious tone Dr. Edge used, but he understood it. Dr. Edge needed someone he could trust. The doctors and/or nurses who were not to be trusted were the ones who would increase the medication of his patient without notification. Tom could not wait to get out of this place, which was starting to seem more like an institution.

Tom got down on his knees and began to pray. He prayed for the doctor's protection, although he wasn't sure why. He got up off his knees and called his wife and prayed again. They knew that none of them would get a good night's sleep, but they would do their best to rest with their eyes closed. Dinner would be served, and then either he or a nurse would make up the rollaway bed, and he would try to get some shut-eye.

# Chapter 6

## *Who's There?*

The next morning, Penny woke to banging at the front door. Silver was barking. Penny thought about Silver's barking, something to which she would have to become accustomed. She thought about the other requirements of a dog owner, such as taking the dog on walks, bathing him, and having veterinarian visits. Despite these things, she had decided that Silver was tradeoff for a little of her time. He offered protection.

The barking continued. She would be grateful for her worthwhile canine friend. As for the moment Silver would have to keep barking. She didn't have time to play with him or take him for a walk; she needed to see who was at the front door. It did not register with her that he was barking because someone was knocking at the front door.

The gun was overkill. She thought about getting it off the top shelf of her closet, but it was much too early in the morning to be shooting people. She smiled to herself at her own sense of humor. Silver would have to do. She grabbed her robe and slipped it over her pjs. Penny pulled her bedroom door open to find Jasmine standing there.

She wore a long-sleeved, cotton blend, blue, teddy bear pajama set that hung loosely on her darkskin while her black hair was pulled back into a ponytail. It was altogether a different look than Penny was used to seeing. Jasmine's outfit would have been cute if it wasn't accompanied by her long-drawn face with slits for eyes. What was worst was her attitude. " I think we should pretend we're not home. After all, it's six thirty in the morning. I looked through the blinds, and it's an elderly couple, probably one of your neighbors. I don't mind being neighborly. But you never know who's going nuts and who's not," said Jasmine.

Penny would have laughed, but she looked at Jasmine, whose face was expressionless and realized she was serious. It registered that Jasmine may not be a morning person like herself.

Samuel opened his door. Samuel had a similar set of pajamas—except that his pjs were a darker blue with yellow ducks. The fifties-style collars on both Jasmine and Samuel's nightshirts were the same though. Samuel, who had heard their conversation, through in his opinion. "Zombies don't knock, so it's probably just a neighbor of yours," he ventured Samuel, like every young boy in his neighborhood, according to his mother, had a fixation with zombies. She said it was evident at their Halloween block party when it was as if their neighborhood only had the "undead" for their children.

Penny had already passed him in the hall. "No kidding," she said as she flipped her head around and let it awkwardly fall to her shoulder. She opened her mouth and eyes wide to make her best impression of a zombie face. After she finished grunting, she became somber. Samuel was still laughing. She looked at Jasmine to nudge her to help with Samuel. Jasmine went and put her hand on his shoulder. "All the same, Samuel, neighbor or zombie, I need you to stay here."

Samuel did not listen and followed his aunt down the hallway but stopped where the hallway met the foyer. Jasmine waited at the end of the hallway with Samuel.

Penny looked through the peephole. Penny recognized her neighbors, although she wasn't sure exactly where they lived on her street. She opened the door. "Hi, Beverly, Jag. To what do I owe the honor?" she asked, definitely a morning person.

Jasmine and Samuel emerged from the hallway.

Jag and Beverly looked at each other and then at Penny, Jasmine, and Samuel. "We've been very startled by something," Jag said. "Are Kelso or Tom around? Kelso, who we just officially met a couple of days ago, was kind enough to assist us in understanding things are changing. Tom, his friend, left us with his phone number. We tried to contact him, but we haven't been able to get in touch with him. It may be our cell phone. We sometimes lose signal out here. Anyway, the strangest thing happened last night. We were watching our television set and eating a little dinner when we heard the doorbell ring. We got up to answer the door, but no one was there. So we sat back down to finish our dinner." Jag looked around outside. "Can we come in?" he asked.

Jasmine wished that Penny had listened to her and ignored them, even though their story was starting to be of interest.

Penny was intrigued and immediately got goose bumps. "Sure, please come in," she said. "Have a seat. I can't wait to hear the rest of your story, but it may have to wait a few minutes. I'm going to change real quick and brew some coffee. I'll use our French press. Would you like some? I also have decaf, but I would have to make that individually. I only have single pods for decaffeinated coffee."

Beverly exchanged a disapproving look with Jag. "What we have to say really cannot wait. We would like to get on with our story if possible," said Jag.

Penny needed to be dressed before her day was to begin at such a rushed pace. "I want to be in something other than my pjs in case someone else drops by. Who knew I would have visitors so early in the morning? You may not be the only ones to stop by to see us." she said trying to lighten the mood.

The curtains that hung in the front window which overlooked the front porch were pulled back. She peeked out the window before opening the front door and let Silver out onto their lawn. He galloped to the end of the perimeter of the yard and started to sniff the ground for a place to do his business. Penny closed the door and smiled at Beverly and Jag. She then made her way down the hallway to change out of her nighttime attire.

The couple sat down in the living room on the leather sofa. "We are sorry for the intrusion, really we are, but Tom and Kelso wanted us to be safe. By the way, where are they?" asked Beverly.

Jasmine sat down on a flowered print, custom upholstered chair a few feet from the matching loveseat for a sofa.

Samuel stood next to Jasmine. He glanced down at

his pajamas and then at Jasmine's pajamas. Samuel politely excused himself, since he thought he should also be out of his pajamas. He waited for Jasmine to pardon herself as he walked away, but Jasmine continued to just sit in her chair and stare. "You should change too," he said to Jasmine, giving her a look as he lifted his collar.

Jasmine lifted her eyebrows. Samuel repeated his words. "You should go get dressed, too," he said with more authority. He did not want to miss any of the story.

Jasmine shoed him away with her hand and told the couple the whereabouts of Tom and Kelso.

Silver barked from outside the door. Jasmine, whose feet were dangling comfortably over the chair, got up and went to the door to let Silver in. Silver pranced to the door and then to his water dish. After he finished lapping up water, he sniffed his empty food dish. Jasmine, who had followed the dog into the kitchen, found the dog food on the counter and filled the dish generously. Jasmine got herself a glass of water and refilled the dog's water dish. She casually walked back to where Beverley and Jag eagerly awaited their audience.

Meanwhile, Penny brushed her teeth, showered, and dressed quickly. She avoided eye contact as she walked past Jasmine, and the older couple into the kitchen. She sidestepped Samuel, who stood in the foyer staring defiantly at Jasmine.

Penny pulled out the coffee pot from under the counter and plugged it in. She then opened up the cupboard and pulled out some filters and gourmet ground coffee. She had originally thought she would use her new French press that she'd ordered online last Christmas but had decided, since everyone was in such a hurry, she would just brew coffee the old fashion way. Although it was not exactly "old fashioned," she thought, since the French press had been around since the 1920s and the coffee pot, drip brewing, had really only became popular in the 1970s, replacing the old coffee percolator. Anyway, it would still be a good cup of Joe, she thought to herself, even if she did not press the ground coffee herself.

Jasmine, who had rejoined everyone in the living room, excused herself and came into the kitchen. "Is everything all right? Is there anything I can do to help?" she asked. She came close to Penny's side to see what she was doing.

Penny finished preparing the coffee. It started to brew slowly. "Doesn't coffee smell good?" Penny said as she lifted the bag of coffee grounds to her nose and then to Jasmine's, "especially in the morning. Would you mind grabbing that box of blueberry muffin mix in that cabinet?" Penny asked and pointed.

The small box was an unknown brand. *Is she really making muffins, or will it be her famous blueberry coffee cake? Doesn't she know how anxious her guests are to finish their story?* Jasmine thought to herself. Penny again pointed but this time to Jasmine's nose. Jasmine had ground coffee on it which she wiped off.

Jasmine obeyed Penny's directive and, after guessing at the wrong cabinet, found the muffin mix in the next cabinet. She studied the box for a minute before handing it to Penny. The blueberries were in the flour mixture instead of in a can within the box. "Aren't you curious about Beverly and Jag? They seem a little anxious to tell their story and are a bit out of sorts. If you would like, I could finish up for you," Jasmine whispered.

Food made sense and not nonsense. "No, this is what I do in the mornings. I understand that they need to get to the bottom of whatever they experienced, but Samuel and I need to eat. I will use the leftovers from yesterday's breakfast, which should help on time. But I also want to make something freshly baked. I'll add my own blueberries their mixture. It is one of Samuel's favorites. This will only take me a minute. The total baking time is?". She paused for Jasmine's attention while reading at the box. "It'll take less than twenty minutes, and then everyone can have my undivided attention while they eat." said Penny as she leaned her head over and to see her neighbors patiently sitting on the sofa.

Beverly waved. Penny waved back.

The recipe called for preheating the oven. "Could you turn on the oven and set it to 350 degrees?" asked Penny. She had taken the box from Jasmine and poured into the pan after she had sprayed with olive oil and added the other measured ingredients, an egg and fresh blueberries. She then mixed them together.

The pan was half-full. "Gluten free if you can believe it. It is good for the abdomen. We won't wait for the oven to preheat since we are in a hurry. It doesn't bake too unevenly."

The next step was anticipated. The oven door was opened. Penny slid the pan into the oven, and Jasmine closed it.

Penny set down three empty coffee cups with saucers on the counter. The coffeemaker was still brewing when she poured herself a cup of coffee. It would be the strongest cup of coffee in the pot. Samuel came into the kitchen to show her that he was dressed but gave Jasmine the side-eye.

Penny gave him a hug and smelled his breath. "Now, please go and brush your teeth and wash your face." She turned him around and sent him in the other direction. He could shower tomorrow so it will feel more like a holiday, she thought and smiled to herself.

Penny followed him out of the kitchen and joined her neighbors. She glanced over her shoulder at Jasmine. Jasmine had found the largest coffee mug they owned and had proceeded to the coffee pot.

Penny quickly sat in the chair Jasmine had been seated in across from Beverly and Jag. She placed her coffee cup on the floor beside her. She folded her hands in her lap. "Would you like to finish your story in the kitchen with some fresh coffee?" asked Penny as she leaned into the couple.

Mary Poppins came to mind as they waited for their host. "Sure we can do that," said Jag as he stood up and held out his hand to help his wife up. "But I have to let you know that this is important."

They started to follow her into the kitchen, and their cell phone rang. It was Tom calling them back. Beverly immediately started speaking. She was excited to talk with Tom and started in the middle of their story, which seemed to confuse everyone who was listening to her talk.

Penny pulled out the kitchen chairs from the table to show them where they could sit. She then retrieved the coffee cups and saucers from the counter and set them on the table. She put the coffee in a carafe and placed it on a pot warmer in the middle of the table.

Samuel, who'd finished brushing his teeth and washing his face, sat next to Beverly and Jag, waiting to be fed. Penny stuck the frozen pancakes from the previous morning in the toaster and heated up some bacon in the microwave and served it to Samuel. Penny also put additional pancakes next to the blueberry coffee cake in the oven. She put bacon, cream, sugar, and some syrup in the center of the table. She added the pancakes as soon as they were warmed up. Jasmine, who sat on a bar stool at the counter, fixed a plate of fruit. She added the fruit to the assembly of items in the middle of the table. She joined everyone at the kitchen table after retrieving her large cup of coffee from the counter, which she was now was holding with both hands.

Jag, now sitting down, held out his hand to Beverly. Beverly put the cell phone in the palm of his hand. He brought the phone to his ear and started to speak. "We're glad to hear from you," he said. "Did we wake you with the phone calls? First, we had tried to text you a message, actually several messages. I'm not sure if we did it right."

Beverly was busy fixing Jag's coffee, along with a small plate of fruit, bacon, and leftover pancakes. Samuel was no longer listening to Beverly and Jag's story but eating his stack of pancakes loaded with strawberries and homemade whipped cream that his aunt had fixed for him.

Tom switched his phone from his ear to his hand and checked his text messages as they were talking. "Yes, I got them. You texted me "911" three times. There were people outside of your house, and they were looking in your windows. They knocked on the door and also rang the doorbell, but when you went to answer the door, nobody was there. You wrote, 'They trampled our garden.' Oh, I see." Tom said as he read on. "Eventually they went away after trampling your garden by the kitchen." Tom read the messages verbatim but was getting frustrated. "OK, so just tell me what happened," he said.

"We went to see who was at the front door, but there was no one there. We thought maybe it was some kids playing a prank, but there aren't many kids who live on our street. During Halloween, we never get trick-or-treaters."

Tom made a face as he tried to make sense of all the texts, which he still had not finished reading.

"It started with the doorbell. It rang only once and nobody was there. Then later there was a knock on the door. It was a weird knock. It was as it they used a rock or something. It was a thump and then scraping," Jag said.

Beverly looked at him and smiled. "It wasn't exactly like that," she said. "I don't remember there being any scraping at the front door, just a couple of thumps. That is, not until someone tried to come in the back door through the garden. Then I seem to remember something scraping against one of the windows. I am so glad we remembered to lock that back door. It is a blessing," said Beverly.

Jag made an unhappy face at Beverly. "Are you going let me finish telling him what happened?" he asked. "Or do you want to tell him? You did not do such a great job the first time." Jag looked a little perturbed.

Beverly shook her head and waved her hand for him to continue.

Penny put up her index finger as a sign to Jag as if she

was supposed to be part of the phone conversation with Tom. She was signaling to him to wait for her to come back to the table so she could listen to their conversation. She left the table and went over to Samuel, who had finished eating breakfast and was now sitting in the great room playing on his phone. Penny laid her hands on his shoulders and squatted down to be eye level with him. "Samuel, I need you to go to another room for a little bit. Could you go to your room?" she asked.

Samuel obeyed and got up off of the ground.

Penny escorted Samuel out of the room. As she passed by the antique table in the foyer, she opened the drawer and pulled out her iPad. She pulled up Jumping Birds, one of the only games she had on it and handed it to Samuel. He slowly walked down the hallway to his room. She went back to her seat and sat down, motioning for Jag to continue his story.

Jag had been explaining to Tom what they had seen when Penny sat down. "We eventually saw the visiting vagrants tromp through our backyard unaware of my wife's gardening underfoot. They may have even taken some bites out of the raw vegetables and fruit that grew in our garden. We shouted at them to go away, but they paid no attention; they looked right through us. It was if they were on drugs or ill, or they just didn't care. It was as if they were in the between phase of life and death. They had an usual hue to their skin and were seemingly in poor coordination."

The answer came slowly. "No, we're safe now. We're at your house. Actually, at Kelso's and …" Jag paused and stared at Penny. "What's your name?"

Beverly answered for Penny. Jag repeated her name in possessive form.

Tom, who was now anxious to talk to his wife, tried to hurry Jag along with the story. "So, you had people wandering through your yard. Did they ever leave? Did you call the police? How did you leave things, Jag?" he asked.

Jag felt as if Tom was treating him like he was stupid. He tried not to lose his temper. "Well that's the thing, Tom. I did call the police. They said that too many people are migrating from the city for safety reasons. The police department could not control the populace or traffic of the thoroughfares. Then he also added that, if it wasn't something significant—murder or a large theft—they wouldn't even try to come out. But the National Guard was working on stationing persons in different areas of the towns," said Jag.

Penny was becoming a little frightened and started to feel overwhelmed again. She got up and pulled the hot pan of blueberry coffee cake out from the oven and set it directly on a hot plate on the kitchen table. Jasmine, who had been enjoying her yogurt, fruit, and cup of coffee at the kitchen table, listened intently. She exchanged looks with Penny as they remembered the wanderers they had seen yesterday on the road. Jasmine shook her head.

Beverly whispered in Jag's ear to continue.

"The worst of it wasn't the hungry people wondering through our yard or having that feeling of helplessness," said Jag. "It was concern for who those people are. They were the guests of the Kilkennys. I'm almost sure of it. The Kilkennys have cancer. Mrs. Kilkenny beat it, five years cancer free, but Mr. Kilkenny is still undergoing treatment. Anyway, their friends are some of the people we met through some of the events they host to raise money. Again, I'm almost sure of it. I went over there to see how they were faring, and I couldn't find anyone. But the cars of their guests were still parked there. I left phone messages for the Kilkennys, but no one answered. They're gone, but their friends are still around. Isn't that strange?"

Tom told Jag they would get to the bottom of things and asked if he would not mind taking the phone off of speakerphone and handing the phone to Jasmine, his wife, so he could talk with her privately. Jag turned around and held out his phone for Jasmine to take.

Jasmine stopped eating. She leaned forward, took the phone from his hand, and put it close to her ear. "Hi. I miss you, too." she said.

Tom, on the other end of the phone, smiled. "I miss you, too. We have to do some brainstorming next time we talk. But for now, could you check out the Kilkennys' house?"

Jasmine pulled the phone from her ear and repositioned the phone in front of her mouth. "Tom, I don't think it's safe. Penny and I went for a run yesterday morning and saw those same people, and they didn't look well." Jasmine put the phone back to her ear and continued. "Penny and I were scared that we could become infected or something. Some of their actions and behavior may make sense if some of them were sick with cancer. But obviously there's something else to it besides post-chemotherapy cognitive impairment, chemo brain. I'm not making excuses, Tom, but I don't want to be exposed. There are also other people to consider besides myself."

"They might be dead, Jasmine. Can you try calling over there? And if no one picks up, try the police again and tell them you suspect foul play. You don't have to expose yourself," said Tom. He was usually right about these things. "I wish I was there to help you out. I have a feeling that things are just as weird here as they are there. Let's have faith that the Lord is still with us in our bizarre circumstances."

"I have faith. I do, but I am not going to put myself in a precarious situation," Jasmine replied. "I'll give Jag back his phone and call the Kilkennys. Can we say a quick prayer?"

They prayed for the Kilkennys, the wandering vagrants, Jag and Beverly, their families, and their own protection. Jasmine so wanted to tell him to come home, but she couldn't do it. She sometimes resented him for always trying to do the right thing. Now was one of those times.

Penny came over to be by Jasmine's side. She had heard their prayer and silently prayed too. She didn't know if it was right or not, but she always felt better after she prayed. She again wished for faith. It was like Jasmine had hidden strength that she could not access from anywhere else but Him.

# Chapter 7

## Time to Go

Kelso was half listening to Tom's conversation as he lay in bed. "Amen," he said. "You got a prayer for me?"

Tom laughed. "You were included."

"No really. I feel like dog poop. I feel like my head has been hit over and over with a sledgehammer, my eyes are going to pulsate out of my head, and I can't focus." As he said this, Kelso lowered his bed and put his feet on the floor. Tom noticed he was dizzy and offered to help him out of bed, but Kelso declined. Kelso was anything but macho, but he knew he had to become self-sufficient quickly.

Kelso found himself to be very unstable as he wobbled over to the side of the bed, where a pitcher of water had been left by one of the nurses. He grabbed a glass and poured some water. He had the cup of water in one hand while holding onto the pole his IV bag was attached to with the other. He chugged the water and then he poured another one; he drank a total of seven cups of water.

He then took some baby steps toward the bathroom. He put the water in the other hand and slowly turned the knob of the bathroom door as he pushed his pole to the same side of the door and looked back at Tom and smiled. "See, Mom, I can do this."

Tom grinned and shook his head.

Tom related to Kelso what was happening with his neighbors, Beverly and Jag, through the bathroom door. Puking noises emanated from the bathroom.

"Are you all right?" asked Tom.

"Not to worry, I think I'm just getting some of the extra medication out of my system," Kelso said kiddingly as he wished he hadn't drank so much water. He drew closer to the toilet and noticed that blood was part of the mixture. He decided not to say anything until he understood more. There was an unexplainable peace that came over him. He knew he should be worried, but instead, he thanked God for the prayer that had been said for him.

Kelso stood up from his bent-over position and rinsed and wiped his mouth. He flushed the toilet and continued to speak. "They must have been really scared, especially if the police didn't think they could make it out that way. It's times like this I wish we knew more of our neighbors. What a disappointment; we said we would be there for them and we're not. And if I know Penny, I'm sure she tried, but she is anything but neighborly. She absolutely hates block parties and the like. I think she's probably telling them they need to rough it out from their own home. She's especially territorial around Samuel," said Kelso through the door.

"Jasmine likes to keep to herself as well," Tom said as he consumed more of the contagion information that was sent to him by Jasmine. "I have a feeling that this virus and/or bacterial illness is more infectious than we realize. I'm texting Jasmine as we speak. I'm going to let her know that Beverly and Jag need to stay with them until we get back. Also, Jasmine was right. She should stay put and not investigate until we get back—although I do think something is up at the Kilkennys."

Just then, Nurse Bratchet lightly knocked and opened the door to their room.

Nurse Bratchet put two breakfast trays on the table. She shut the door behind her. Tom knew it wasn't the normal protocol for a nurse to shut the door unless there was some invasive procedure she was about to do. "Nurse Bratchet, always a pleasure. Thank you for getting me to bed last night. I slept wonderful. How can we be of service to you?" said Tom. He had noticed that certain people at the hospital had started to grow on him, some in a good way and some in other ways.

The nurse smiled at Tom as she found a place for their breakfast trays. "Is Kelso in the bathroom?" she asked in a superficial and calm tone.

Tom nodded yes.

She came close to the bathroom door. Tom was going to stop her from going in, but she stopped with her hand on the doorknob. Nurse Bratchet put her head close to the crack where the door met the door frame.

The nurse moved her hand from the doorknob to the door. "You young men need to get out of here now. Though I'm not at liberty to say, I will say it anyway. This hospital may go on lockdown. Parts of Central, which is much bigger than our humble hospital, already are on lockdown." Nurse Bratchet paused as if she was listening to the voices in the hallway.

Tom put down his phone. She continued to speak in a low monotone voice. "We don't know when it may happen, and we're not even sure why. But there've been many harmless cases of people getting out of their beds and wandering aimlessly around the halls in different wards. This is not so out of the ordinary except that there are more wanderers than typical, and they are a little less lucid, which I attribute to their high temperatures. Still other patients are listless with the flu virus but only a low-grade temperature. Hospital officials and doctors are particularly concerned with either a bacterial infection or the virus. But no one is talking."

Tom immediately jumped to his feet and started to get their things together. He wondered if his car would still be where it was parked a couple of streets away. As Kelso opened the door, Nurse Bratchet noticed the vomit smell. She then positioned herself under Kelso's arm. As they made their way back to bed, another nurse who was not on either Kelso's or Tom's good side entered the room. It was Nurse Hiho, the head nurse of the unit.

Nurse Bratchet and the head nurse exchanged smiles. Nurse Hiho assumed that Nurse Bratchet was helping out on their floor because she had been reassigned, and she had not yet looked at the morning roster. Either way, there was much to do, as the hospital was still overloaded. She told Nurse Bratchet about another patient up the hall who needed his bedpan emptied, which usually was a volunteer's job but not today. Normally she would have immediately exited the room but again not today.

Kelso pretended to be very sleepy and medicated. Nurse Hiho was insistent on hooking up another IV with more pain medication, but Tom interceded. He refused to let her, citing Dr. Edge.

She turned to Kelso. "I know you're in pain. Do you want to take some pain medication orally and not intravenously?" she asked. "That would be OK according to your current chart."

Nurse Hiho looked down at a piece of paper she had in her hand. "You will want and need more pain medication throughout the day. Doctor's orders, not Dr. Edge's but Dr. Keller's. I have his handwritten notes as an addendum in my possession." She lifted a piece of paper and attached it to the back of Kelso's chart. She then scribbled the new prescription onto the chart itself.

Kelso still faked being highly medicated and half asleep, although the chart reflected his current level of medication, which was nil. It was debatable as to how much pain medication was actually in his system. Kelso decided to put his act in overdrive. Kelso started to mumble various names of characters from the Harry Potter series.

Kelso started with the head wizard, Dumbledore. "Dumbledore, is that you? No, it can't, be you? Ron Weasley, Harry, Hermione … Snipe. Tell me it isn't so." Kelso as he repeated the names over and over, with a few additional obscure Harry Potter character names.

Tom wasn't sure how wise it was to antagonize this particular nurse and turned his face toward the window. Nurse Bratchet did the same.

Nurse Hiho looked around the room, first at Tom and

then at Nurse Bratchet. Nurse Bratchet now stared down at their breakfast trays. She knew Nurse Hiho was looking at her for support. She wished she had left the room when she'd had the chance.

Kelso was exhausting Nurse Hiho's patience. "I would like to exercise my right and say no to drugs. Have you ever seen a brain on drugs? It looks like fried eggs," Kelso said, amused. "Also Dr. Edge is my doctor, not anyone else." This time he used a sterner tone.

Kelso thought about letting another IV quietly drip into his subconscious, but for now, he decided to stick to the plan of going cold turkey, which would not be trouble free. He wished he did not have to feel the burning or nausea in the pit of his stomach. He would prefer not to deal with the constant ache in his side, not to mention the drum-thumping headache or the aching of his bones. But onward he would trudge. They needed to get out of this place quickly.

"You have a weird sense of humor, Mr. Brandon. I will check with Dr. Edge, but I know that Dr. Keller will not be pleased. He was asked to step in and help with Kelso's treatment plan. I am leaving these pills for you in case you change your mind." The nurse left the pain medication in a small white paper cup on the tray beside the water pitcher. "I'll be back," she said and paused for a second. "I was never a fan of Harry Potter, too many witches." She left the door open behind her.

Tom went and confiscated the pain pills for later. "I'm glad to see that Mr. Kelso Brandon has taken all his pain medication. I'll make note of it on the chart," Nurse Bratchet said. She needed to let them know one more important piece of information but could not risk anyone overhearing. She moved the breakfast tray out of the way. "This should do it. Enjoy!" she said and left the room as another nurse walked in.

Nurse Poohe approached Kelso. She was to check his vitals again. Kelso was really starting to hate hospitals, as the procedures seemed to get more and more intrusive. *Maybe I'm just special.*

Nurse Poohe grabbed his wrist and started to count to herself. When she was done, she wrote down a number. After she was finished taking his vitals, she moved his breakfast tray in front of him. "Thanks, nurse … What's your name?" Kelso asked, even though he could read her name tag.

"My last name is pronounced *Pow*, like a punch in the face. It's not like it looks for Americans," said Nurse Poohe.

Tom, who could also read her nametag, made a hmmm sound of acknowledgement.

"I see you took your medication after all. Good for you." She poured him some water.

Nurse Hiho had sent Nurse Poohe specifically to take his vitals but, more importantly, to convince him to take the pain medication. They were under Dr. Keller's orders to keep a close eye on Kelso Brandon. Dr. Keller did not want him to leave the hospital anytime soon.

"Yes, I'm feeling OK and doing well on the medication," said Kelso. "Dr. Edge is making sure I get well quickly. He's the one who suggested I meet him at this hospital." He wanted to had the adjective *forsaken* but kept it to himself.

"Those pills that you just took should make you a little sleepy. We also would like to start another drip for you," suggested the nurse.

Tom said, "No." And Kelso shook his head in agreement with Tom.

Nurse Poohe was not pleased. "The drip would be for pain medication, but it would be on a very low amount since you are already medicated. Our orders from Dr. Keller are to put you on this medication so you can rest; you need to heal. You wouldn't want that spleen to rupture within the next couple of days that you're here. I don't think you'll be here much longer than that." She was unaware of any proposed lockdown.

Kelso looked sicker than usual. Now beyond a shadow of a doubt, he knew something was up with regards to him being able to leave the hospital. There was a reason they wanted to keep him in the hospital. He drank the water. "My doctor is Dr. Edge. I don't know who Dr. Keller is or why he has been assigned as a second physician by the hospital. Do you have any other information?"

Nurse Poohe knew Mr. Brandon's case was a little suspicious, but it was not for her to speculate.

Tom repeated the question.

Nurse Poohe had the same question herself but answered Kelso's and Tom's question without a hiccup. "That is correct, but Dr. Edge is too busy making rounds. Dr. Keller is one of attending doctors on call and a specialist in pathology. He is filling in where he is needed. He is a very good physician, famous in fact. You are quite lucky to have him," she said. "Now try to get some rest."

She'd started to close the door behind her when she said, "Speak of the devil."

Dr. Keller walked into the room and picked up the chart; he looked at both men and smiled. "We will need another sample of your blood at noon, and the lab will work up a full analysis to see if any toxins have entered your system from the bacterial infection. This will also let us know how the spleen is doing," Dr. Keller said without properly introducing himself.

It was obvious that Dr. Keller was quite preoccupied. Kelso tried to act sleepy but decided he was not in the mood and to play it straight.

"Oh, I am sorry I did not properly introduce myself. I'm Dr. Keller. I am head of Neurology and Neurosciences at Stanford. I'm also a specialist in pathology. I don't usually attend here but am here out of necessity. I'm also helping out with some of the doctors' rounds."

Kelso thought about what he had said—that he was here out of necessity and he was helping out with rounds. "It sounds like there's an epidemic, Dr. Keller, and you are trying to get to the bottom of it. Am I part of the 'necessity' of you being here or 'doctor's rounds'?" he asked.

Tom quickly threw the pieces together. He knew it was not the "doctor's rounds" and that they now were in the heart of a possible pandemic.

Dr. Keller studied them both. The last thing the doctor wanted was for Kelso to know they suspected him to be in the early or latent stage of this disease. "I am helping out Dr. Edge. I am a specialist. And may I say, Mr. Brandon, you are lucky you were even admitted when you were and even luckier that we found this infection. Do you feel like you have lost any feeling in your arms, legs, or any other locations?" asked Dr. Keller.

The doctor was glad when Kelso said no. "I'm going to test your reflexes," he said, moving the breakfast tray out of the way.

"Sure, no problem," said Kelso. Kelso thought about how he may just land a right cross to Dr. Keller's face to let him know that his reflexes were working well enough.

He sat on the side of the bed as the doctor examined his legs and tapped on his knees. He talked into his microphone and noted that there were no signs of paralysis, nerve damage, or muscle atrophy. Kelso could not believe this doctor was for real.

"Your reflexes are normal. You feel no numbness anywhere in your body or shooting pains in your arms or legs?" asked Dr. Keller, repeating part of an earlier question.

Kelso shook his head. He was anxious to exit the hospital as quickly as possible before they got caught in lockdown. He thought about a pain in his neck, but it would be relieved as the doctor made his way out.

"OK then." The doctor sounded disappointed but looked relieved at the same time. "Go back to sleep. That medication you took will make you very sleepy. I will come back to check on you in an hour or two."

"Thank you, Doctor," Kelso said. He slid his legs back onto the bed.

The doctor pulled the cover over his legs, which gave Kelso the chills. Kelso pulled the blanket closer to his chest. It was if he was in his childhood days and he was being tucked in by one of his parents. The part that was missing was the bedtime story. But for now, he'd heard quite enough—ample enough to give him and Tom both nightmares.

"I will tell the nurses to leave you alone if possible so you can rest. At least a solid hour should help. Sleep is the best medicine." Dr. Keller wished for some of his own.

"Thanks, Doctor," Kelso said as he closed his eyes.

As soon as the doctor closed the door, Kelso gave a what-the-heck look to Tom. "I have a big target on my head. How am I going to get out of here?" he asked. His heart started to race.

Tom got Kelso's clothes together and handed them to him. Just then, Nurse Bratchet opened the door. "Sorry, I'm not supposed to be in here. Godspeed," she said. As they watched, she held up a note with her right hand and dropped it on the floor as she shut the door.

Tom grabbed the note and read it in a low voice to Kelso. "The note reads: 'You are not to leave the hospital as far as the hospital officials are concerned, although I do not believe that it is limited to hospital officials. They are flying in other scientists and specialists from all over the country. The pathology department is now classified, and you need classified access to enter. It's your blood. Something is in it. The previous workup of your blood tissue showed some signs of a carcinogen that may be linked a certain pathogen. I don't know much more than that.'" Tom could not believe what he was reading.

Tom stopped. He looked at Kelso.

"And? Keep on reading. I'm OK," said Kelso. "I'm going to be ok. You think you're the only one with a little faith?"

Tom's hand started to shake out of fear or anger, but he continued to read. He held the paper a little lower so the shaking wasn't visible. "'They're trying not to violate your rights but need answers. I don't know much more, but I'm getting bits and pieces from some social websites. Dr. Edge wanted me to watch out for you and had the same sentiments. Take care and get out while you still can. Otherwise, you and Tom could become infected like some of the rest of us.'"

Tom looked up at Kelso. Kelso was still white. He handed Kelso some of the hand sanitizer he had squirted from the bottle next to the box of Kleenexes. He wasn't sure anymore who needed it most, them or everyone else.

# Chapter 8

## The Kilkennys

*J*asmine climbed over the fence of the Kilkennys property. She looked around but saw no one. She'd left Penny at home clearing dishes from breakfast, not letting on that she was headed to the Kilkennys. As Jasmine arrived at the back of the house, she noticed the screen door was open but the main door to the kitchen was locked. The kitchen door had a deadbolt as well as a keyed lock. *It would be easier to access without the deadbolt*, she thought to herself, *just slide and turn*. She put her hands together and stretched her arms over her head.

Jasmine listened for voices through the door but heard none. If she had heard anyone, she would have turned around and headed home without risking being seen, infected, or exposed. Jasmine only wanted to make observations.

So far, Jasmine did not like what she saw, but she needed to keep going before drawing any hard conclusions. She preferred to find an unlocked window or at least one she could see through before she thought about breaking and entering, which was a felony for which she would not be caught. She hoped she could make a quick assessment of the Kilkennys' situation without having to go into the house. If she could get entrance through one of the windows she would be able to detect whether there had been foul play. She crouched down and stretched out her back. Stretching helped her to focus.

Jasmine had already assessed from the outside that no one had broken into the house; everything seemed to be in place just as if someone was at home. No windows were broken or jimmied. There was only one car parked under the carport, and no stains on the pavement suggested that they owned another car. *But still something is off,* she thought to herself.

Jasmine had started in the direction of the nearest window when she heard someone in the front yard. She wondered if she had been spotted.

"Down on your knees!" yelled the policeman who ran up behind her.

Jasmine wondered if this had been such a good idea after all, but her conscience had told her she needed to check on the Kilkennys. And who was better suited for the job? It was what Tom would do if he was in the same situation. She walked back onto the carport and followed the officer's instructions, kneeling to the ground with hands behind her head. She felt like a fool.

The officer looked at Jasmine's demeanor and realized it wasn't likely she was breaking into the house. He helped her to her feet. "Do you live here or did you come to visit the Kilkennys? We had reports of suspicious behavior and perhaps foul play," said the policeman. He then turned and yelled to his partner to continue to the front of the house.

Jasmine looked at the officer and said a quick prayer. *Foul play* seemed unlikely, but the words resonated in her thoughts. Jag must have called the police again after she'd left the house as Tom had suggested she do during their phone call. She wished Jag had not made that second call. *Now I may not get any answers*, she thought to herself.

She saw his name tag, Officer John Stamos. She decided not to call him Officer Stamos until he introduced himself, which he did. She could now fall back on her people skills. She soon hoped to have all the information on Officer Stamos that she would need for any future reference.

"I actually am glad you're here, Officer Stamos. I was just worried about the Kilkennys. I'm not sure where they are at. since they haven't answered their phone, and their car is parked under the carport." Jasmine was aware that she had never actually met the couple and was skirting the truth. She didn't think it was wise to volunteer any information about any of the people back at the house, so she decided to take on a new persona. She would be Beverly, someone well established in the community and solely acting on her own interests.

Jasmine did a quick estimation of what was next and exactly how long it would take. She would be asked some questions and told to stick around while they investigated. But she had another agenda for the officer's interrogation; she needed some of her own intel. The best way for her to get local information was still an old-fashioned conversation—especially if one of them happened to be well connected to the community, like Officer Stamos.

Jasmine had noticed her mainstream sources of news were now becoming contaminated with censorship. Certain live footage was no longer being posted. And although she knew how to hack into satellite feeds, in doing so, there was a small chance that her location could be compromised. Jasmine needed to know what facilities, transportation locations, and roadways were safe and still viable. Most of this information could easy come from a police radio or, even better, a policeman.

John stared at Jasmine for a few seconds. He didn't trust her; she just didn't look that neighborly. If he had her pegged right, she did not belong in any suburb but, rather, in the heart of the city. He usually wasn't wrong about people. But in this circumstance, he didn't care where she lived; he just had to figure out what had happened to the Kilkennys.

Jasmine wanted to get in her questions first before he realized he was off target. "How is it out there? Is it safe to travel?" she asked.

She was thinking that it was unbearably hostile. John confirmed it.

John was put at ease by Jasmine's disposition and disarmed by her questions. He was glad to talk to someone who was perceivably "normal." John started to tell Jasmine the things he was experiencing on a personal level as a police officer.

*Bingo*, Jasmine thought to herself as Officer Stamos started to open up to her. She was happy to become his confidant.

John continued. "You'd think you know people, but you don't. People are not civil. They're hunting each other down and their possessions, acting like savages when we don't even know what resources have been depleted. People are in hysteria. People are being murdered for things that haven't even come to pass. There's no water left on any store shelves because everyone's afraid. People are hoarding it and refusing to share, except for the shelters. The shelters are in abundant supply. I'm not sure why." John looked to Jasmine for a reaction but found none.

John again reminded himself that he was probably right about Jasmine as he looked at the most perfect poker face. "People are just dropping their extra water off in front of the building, but in every other situation, people are not behaving correctly. No one is starving, cold, or hungry—not yet anyway. They're not needing for anything. But they act as if they are."

John again stopped and studied Jasmine and wondered if he should continue. He had yet to ask Jasmine about the Kilkennys. But since they had not discovered anything yet, he thought it could wait. "By the way, you don't have to call me Officer Stamos; you can call me John." He smiled and put his hand out.

Jasmine eagerly shook his hand.

John again continued. "We don't have enough manpower to police the city, even with the National Guard."

He paused, but Jasmine did not want him to stop talking and repeated the words "National Guard?" as a question.

"Don't get me started about the National Guard. There's never been a group of people who make the men in blue seem so flawless and professional. What is worse is that people like your neighbors are insisting the police come out to the suburbs to investigate the stupidest occurrences, like other neighbors acting strangely? Again, we don't have enough manpower. We only wish that we did, but this is a time of crisis." The officer knew that the last comment was not aimed at Jasmine, as he doubted she had made any such phone call.

Jasmine knew this was more than a "stupid occurrence." She thought about the information she had been given by Nancy and was curious as to what they would find in the house. She wanted to check it out herself through a closed window. But for her own safety, this worked out better. Any information that was pertinent to the Kilkenny's whereabouts or situation could easily be assessed by the two officers. She knew she should be more concerned for the officers' well-being, but she was just thankful she was not in charge of the situation.

John realized Jasmine was soaking up every word he said. "The reason I'm here is because of a particular call that came into the station last night," he said and paused and saw that Jasmine was still captivated. "At first the call didn't sound important. My captain told me that a man called and wanted to be transferred to Commissioner Dongor. He was an old friend of Commissioner Dongor. But when the caller couldn't be transferred, since the commissioner was out in the field, the man became anxious. He then insisted that someone come out and look in on the Kilkennys. Although the captain could not spare anyone, I volunteered, since I live around here and was headed home anyway."

Jasmine was impressed. He seemed like he was not only humble, but he also sincerely cared.

"It has been a seventy-two-hour stretch. I'm anxious to get home. Officer Jack, the other officer I came with, did not come from our precinct. He actually came from my house and just finished his half-day nap." John chuckled. "He's not my official partner, but he volunteered to meet me here when I decided to investigate. That's why he's not only in street clothes but wearing clothes he sleeps in at night, his blue sweats and a white T-shirt." Again, John chuckled and smiled. He wondered if he was talking so much because he hadn't slept in such a long while. Everything seemed a little funny.

John continued on one last time with his story. "Jack is also a trained officer of the law, but he's from upstate New York. He's just visiting with me and my family. He's been with us for a while. He's been my best friend from elementary school, and I love him like a brother. His pitch-dark-hearted wife recently left him, so he has been really down on himself. He came out before the big one." John's next sentence was interrupted by the sound of breaking glass and a gunshot.

Jasmine was safe from being detained for the moment. The only other option John had other than letting her alone was to handcuff her in the interim. John and Jasmine both knew there was no time. His partner was still inside the house. John looked Jasmine in the eyes and knew she had played him. She had all the information and he had none.

John wished he had got something, anything, out of her. He assessed that she was hardwired to only tell part of any story. It would be iffy if he would be able to get any straight facts. He had figured her for someone who either worked for a government agency or was an accomplice in crime.

The officer put his hand in front of Jasmine, telling her to stay. "Stand against the wall of the house," he yelled. He had wondered if he had made a mistake in trusting her. Was she with the person Jack had just discovered and possibly shot? he wondered to himself.

Jack was a great shot and never missed, but he also never aimed for the head or heart. He always figured he could get off a second shot if necessary. Although they weren't trained to give someone holding a weapon a second chance, Jack never wanted to kill anyone and have that on his conscience.

"Stay here. You are not free to go. Jack?" yelled John at the top of his lungs as he backed up so he could see the front of the house. He looked at Jasmine and pointed to her as a warning to stay put. His gun was drawn and pointed up. He held onto it with both hands as he made his way toward the front of the house.

Jasmine followed orders and quickly faced the side of the house next to the kitchen door under the carport.

John knew Jasmine had information, at least more than she was letting on. She was no neighbor of theirs. But what was he to do? John questioned to himself.

Jasmine had already sized up the situation at hand. She had to decide whether to stick around and find out what happened or take off running. If she didn't take off running, there was a chance she could be infected—if this contagion was even real. Her gut told her it was and that everything in the house was already contaminated.

The more she thought about it, the more she knew what the right thing to do was. She circled around the house to see Jack open the front door inside the house. "John, you got to see this," he said.

Apparently, there was no break-in except by Jack.

John turned and saw Jasmine standing in the front lawn, apparently not a criminal. "You can go. Can I get your number in case I have any more questions?" he asked. While waiting for Jasmine to answer, he turned to Jack and asked him why he had fired a shot.

"Tell me your phone number." said Jasmine.

John told her his phone number.

"Thanks. I will call you."

Normal police protocol was broken. His instincts were usually on point for profiling people. He knew she would call. She just seemed like the type of person to do exactly as she said she would. John turned back to face Jack and assumed she was gone, but only from sight.

She went back to the carport to the kitchen door. She began wiping her prints off everything she had touched. She heard from a distance Jack say, "We found them." She returned to the front yard after she gave a final wipe to the handle of the screen door with part of her shirt. She thought about burning the infected shirt when she got back to Penny and Kelso's house but wondered if that was overly obsessive.

Tom had worked nonstop with her over the years. He'd tried to get her to become less high-strung. Her obsessive behavior was one of those high-strung traits that they worked on together. Jasmine, once again, thought of Tom, her better half, and wished for him. She wondered what had happened to her in the last few years. Of course, it wasn't just Tom; it was also the church and her involvement in the church body. At one time, she would not have cared if she was overly attentive to details. It used to be part of her job. But now she questioned the things she did as to whether they were radical or not. She wondered if she was being a little paranoid. Tom could tell when she needed to relax. He could tell her to stand down when it was necessary. Jasmine found herself reverting to her old ways of fight or flight—both of which she was internationally renowned for.

Jack did not answer John's question at first, as to why he had taken a shot. "You've got to see this, John. I have never seen anything like this. It's the damn dog. I had to shoot it. It's like it was mutant. It could barely crawl on the ground. It was the scariest damn thing I've ever seen. It's as if it's eyes glowed. It was really messed up. It growled and made gargling sounds as it tried to come toward me, rabies?"

Jasmine now listened from the front stoop.

John glanced out the front door to see Jasmine back standing in front of the house. He turned to Jack and said, "Forget about the damn dog. Have you seen the Kilkennys?"

John could not stop staring at the dead dog. "You're right. That doesn't look like a dog. I'm with you; something weird happened to it. It's like its muscles gave way. And look at those abrasions on its skin." John saw where Jack had put a bullet through its heart to save it from any more pain.

Jack was picking up objects and setting them back down. He was searching for clues. Back home in New York, he was hoping to get a detective position, either in narcotics or homicide, in a year or two. He prided himself on his deductive prowess.

There was no broken glass except for the glass he'd broke on the front door to get inside the house. There were no signs of a struggle. But something had taken the couple's lives. He knew that someone had died other than the dog he had shot by the faint stench that lingered around the corner.

Jack looked around for John. "I found them, or at least their smell. They have to be here, but I just can't figure out what happened to the mutant dog. I haven't finished looking through the house. But I have a feeling we will find something soon. This house gives me the heebie-jeebies." There were plates of unfinished food on different end tables. "Why didn't the dog eat the leftover food on these platters?" he asked.

John looked at the dog again and shook his head. "That smell is definitely something dead." It was foul and becoming more pungent.

Jasmine could not smell anything from where she was standing so she assumed she was safe, but she took a couple more steps back.

The smell was too familiar to the men in blue. "I'm starting to feel sick physically," John said as he came across a closed door to a bathroom. He tried the door, but it was locked. He then took a small metal rod with a pick at the end of it from his pocket. He preferred using a pick if possible, as opposed to busting down the door or breaking a window like officers heroically do in all the cop movies.

It was more sleuth-like. "Got it," he said loudly as he put his hand on the doorknob.

John pushed the door open to the half bath. The bodies of Mr. and Mrs. Kilkenny were slumped together with their feet out in front of them. Their backs were against the wall. Their hands were folded on top of each other's, and their heads were tilted as their bodies leaned together. Other than a suicide pact, John could not think of anything that would act so quickly. They'd had time to lock the bathroom door and die in peace—or what seemed like peace. It was definitely one for the detectives.

"They're in here. I'll call it in." John covered his mouth with his arm and shut the door.

John raced back to the front yard to talk with Jasmine, who had answered only one of his questions. He knew whoever the Los Angeles Police Department sent to investigate the crime scene would want to talk with Jasmine directly, but she was out of sight. He looked down on the front stoop to see four words written with stone: "Wash hands and body."

As soon as it became a crime scene, Jasmine was gone. She had stepped into the house to see the dog but stepped back without touching anything or inhaling.

He needed to go home, wash up, and rest. He told Jack, his house guest and partner, it was time to go. They would come back when the LAPD arrived.

# Chapter 9

# Headed Home

Tom decided to survey the perimeter of the hospital floor. He had an uneasy feeling about leaving Kelso. "Kelso, I'm going for a walk," he said, looking at Kelso's eyes, which were no longer dilated.

"I'll be fine. Go," said Kelso. Kelso was in more pain than he wanted to share with Tom, but Tom knew pain and could see it on his face. Kelso would have to suffer through it.

Tom lay Kelso's phone on his chest. "Kelso, if I'm not back in ten minutes, call Dr. Edge. I shared my contact information with you in a text. Actually," said Tom as he grabbed his phone, "what's your code?"

Kelso thought about how weird Tom was at times but wondered if this did not take the cake. Kelso answered, "Its Penny's birthday." He was becoming increasingly annoyed.

Tom typed in the day and month and checked his messages. He swiftly added Dr. Edge's contact information to his list of contacts. "Kelso, all you have to do is say my name or 'Dr. Edge,' and your phone will dial without any notification. Get it? Just hold down the main button. That way, no one needs to know that you're calling me or Dr. Edge." He knew it was overkill.

"I'll be able to hear whatever is going on. I have already texted Dr. Edge. I didn't get anything back. I'm not sure why. I presume he's still around, just busy. Call Jasmine as a last resort, and she can make all this go away. But only call her as a last resort," Tom concluded.

Kelso looked at Tom and his phone. "Are you kidding?" he said. "Just go and don't make me call anyone. Get your intel and come back. Make it quick."

Tom walked out the door, knowing he was going to be followed and perhaps stopped, since patients were now forbidden to wonder the hallways. But he was up to the challenge. He walked out and all eyes were on him.

Two martials started to follow him. But someone in a dark blue suit instructed the martials not to continue in his pursuit. Tom counted guards and martials, cameras, nurses, and exits. But that was where he ceased. If he didn't have an exit strategy, all the numbers in the world wouldn't help.

Tom went to the public restroom on the floor and spotted a nearby freight elevator. After he exited the restroom, he went to the nurses station and asked the nurse on duty if he could add an extra lunch for himself. He explained that there was only one meal form left in the room. "I'll have the vegetarian selection," said Tom, although it really didn't matter to him.

Nurse Kepler said it would not be a problem. He wrote Tom's preference on a Post-it note beside him.

Tom glanced at the paperwork and Post-it notes that Nurse Kepler had on his desk. The nurse covered one of his notes with his right hand. It was written in red and said that Kelso Brandon was special with *special* underlined.

There was a picture of an eye above it. Tom immediately knew that Kelso was on the radar, but he did not see any other written information that would explain why.

Tom thanked the nurse and went back to the room. Tom's incognito surveillance techniques were rusty at best. Still, the federal official who was about to put the hospital on lockdown watched as Tom returned to Mr. Brandon's room and did not find Tom's behavior suspicious or unusual.

Tom gauged that something at the hospital was about to happen. It was important for the hospital officials to keep Kelso there at the hospital, which accounted for the Nurse Kepler's inscription on the Post-it note. Kelso had a bacterial infection and mononucleosis, but that was all Tom knew for sure.

Tom didn't want to assume that Kelso had tested positive for this contagion that was now becoming a pandemic but could not eliminate any possibilities to account for all scenarios. It was possible, he reasoned, that Kelso could be a "ground zero" patient—one of the first to contract the illness. Tom's head started to swim with thoughts of the severity of what that could mean for everyone. But from what he knew of the contagion, Kelso didn't demonstrate the severity of any symptoms and certainly was not endangering anyone's life. If anything, his and Kelso's lives were endangered by staying at the hospital.

Tom played out the situations in his head. He figured there were two ways it could go. Either the hospital would keep them there under a false pretense until the hospital went on lockdown, or they would let Kelso go.

If it was to become a federal matter, then the good of the many could outweigh the good of the few—totally unconstitutional, but it could happen. The fail-safe for government intervention would be to put the hospital on lockdown like Central Hospital. Or as it should be, Kelso and Tom could just walk out and find his car and go home. As Tom thought about the situation, the exit plan quickly fell in place.

Tom walked into the room. Kelso was already in his street clothes. "Great minds think alike; let's go," said Tom.

Tom received a text from Dr. Edge. It gave information on how to get out of the hospital if there was a lockdown. He too had a plan, but if they weren't out before a lockdown, they needed to do a switch.

It was a new plan. "A switch," Tom texted back. "Got it."

Dr. Edge had mapped out a route through a new wing that was under construction. The elevator they would use to escape had exits from both the front and the back sides. To exit to the back, you needed a code. Dr. Edge texted the code, 7402.

Now Tom's rusty reconnaissance came into play. All the counted items—the cameras, nurses, military personnel, doctors, exits, and elevators—came into play.

"Let's go now," said Kelso.

They would leave through the front door of the hospital unless there was a lockdown; then they would exit through the elevator and the part of the building that was under construction.

Dr. Edge was at the nurses' station signing Kelso's

release papers. Some officers and doctors were gathered around him. Some of the doctors were pushing into him as he was trying to fill out the paperwork. One of the hospital officials sternly discouraged Dr. Edge, telling him it was rash at best to release Kelso Brandon and that his reputation and job could be on the line.

Dr. Keller stood over Dr. Edge's shoulder and argued the point of the many verses the few and that, for scientific reasons, as well as his own personal health, it was wrong to sign his release papers. Dr. Edge anticipated Dr. Keller visiting Kelso's room one last time, trying to persuade him to stay. He wondered if Dr. Keller would tell him the truth about the contagion that was spreading throughout the nation.

Dr. Edge noticed someone open the door of Kelso's room and look out. It was Tom. He was going to make a break for it. *It's about time*, Dr. Edge thought to himself.

Dr. Edge knew that some of the guards and officials who were stationed on the third floor were there specifically for Kelso, and they would be watching his room specifically. Dr. Edge shoved a doctor who was standing far too close to him into the guard standing behind him. The guards were too occupied with themselves at that point to think of anything else for a few seconds. He seized the opportunity to turn to the other doctors with his rebuttal as he finished filling out the last form. He slid Kelso's release papers to the nurse below. He lifted up his head and presented his argument: It was unlawful to keep Kelso against his wishes, and if he had treatment that was manageable at home, there was no reason to keep him under care any longer.

Tom was thankful for the momentary diversion. He and Kelso crouched down. Without hesitation, they darted across the floor, not seen by anyone behind the desk, except for one nurse, who saw their attempted getaway. She chose to pay attention to neither the ruckus Dr. Edge was causing or Tom and Kelso's escape. She just wanted to finish her shift work and not have to stay late. Many nurses were being asked to pull double and triple shifts, but she would not; she had already made up her mind.

She looked at Tom and Tom at her, and then she immediately put her head down without saying a word and continued to type on her keyboard without looking at her screen. She was trying to act nonchalant but knew she was typing incoherently; she would correct it in a minute. She did not want to give any hints and call attention to Tom and Kelso.

It was about a minute and a half until the officers pulled themselves together. It was then that two more government officials walked up the stairs and onto the third floor. Dr. Edge smiled. Dr. Keller whispered something to one of the main government officials in charge, who in turn motioned and told another agent to check room 384.

"No, go the other way. It's at the end of the hall," said Dr. Keller.

Dr. Edge pointed in the other direction

"I don't see how you don't see the importance of this. If they are not there …" said Dr. Keller.

Dr. Edge looked superficially perplexed. He tilted his head and said, "If you are referring to Mr. Brandon, why should he be there? He's been released," said Dr. Edge, a little concerned that Kelso and Tom were not out of the building yet.

Three more men came through the staircase, two of them wearing lab coats. Dr. Keller shook his head, already knowing that Kelso and Tom were gone.

The guards looked in room 384 and confirmed that the patient was gone. The nurse who had seen the whole thing looked up from her computer. She role-played as if she was startled by the commotion. She knew no one would ask her any questions if she was surprised by the situation.

The hospital official who was standing by the government official lifted his walkie-talkie and pushed the red button. "Lockdown," he said calmly.

It was immediate. An alarm sounded, and red and white lights in certain locations started to go on. The nurse dismissed herself from the station. She pointed towards the restroom to one of the other nurses on duty, who motioned for her to go but gave her eyes like she was crazy to think of having to go to the bathroom at a time like this. The nurse really went to find the two men.

Meanwhile, Tom and Kelso tried to keep a low profile and were almost at the home stretch. They'd just passed through the glass French doors that led to the main lobby and were about thirty yards from the front door when the alarms went off. The guards started to move toward the front of the hospital. A tiny army of four guards walked to the main entrance. From outside the hospital, patients who were walking in were ushered away from the front doors by military personnel. They fell into zone positions, guarding all the exits and entrances of the hospital.

Tom and Kelso turned around. Kelso could no longer lean on Tom but needed to act like a visitor instead of a patient. He stood up as straight as he could. Tom took one of the pain pills he'd collected from his pocket and gave it to Kelso. Kelso looked up at him, and although he didn't want to take it, he did anyway, in hopes the medication would help him move a little quicker.

Tom had to consult the text Dr. Edge had sent him as to how to get out of the building. He knew he didn't have time on his side. If only he had just a minute or two to think. "Oh no," Tom said as he studied the diagram.

Kelso, who figured himself to be the brains of the situation, looked over Tom's shoulder and read the text. He looked at Tom. "The third floor?" He asked the rhetorical question.

Tom nodded.

"Shit," Kelso responded. He was hoping the pain meds would kick in sooner, rather than later.

They came up one of the medical elevators again to the third floor. As the door opened, they saw the nurse who had let them escape.

"You," she said in a semi-loud voice with a wink that only they could see.

They stepped out of the elevator.

"You should be more careful. Don't you know this is a medical emergency? The hospital is on lockdown. No one is allowed to exit or enter. This elevator is only for authorized personnel and those who need medical attention," she said.

She preceded in an even louder voice. "Visitors are to wait in the lobby or cafeteria." She pointed to the skyway down across the hall. It wasn't the quickest way to the cafeteria or the lobby. In fact, it was more of a roundabout way to either location.

Another nurse who was observing the confrontation tilted her head when she pointed towards the skywalk.

The helpful nurse turned around in time to see the other nurse get up from her station. "Listen, apparently you don't have much time. The skyway will lead you to the elevators that have the door on the other side that opens to a new wing. It's still undergoing construction and leads to outside the hospital."

Tom checked his text from Dr. Edge, and she was confirming exactly the instructions he had written. He offered up a prayer of thanks for this woman who stood before him.

"I don't have the code, but you may run into somebody who does. I pray that is the case. Be careful," she said.

"Thank you, Marianne," said Tom, reading her name tag, Marianne Hobbs, and mentally adding her to his prayer list.

Tom and Kelso quickly turned around and walked toward the skyway.

*If only they had a little more time*, the nurse thought to herself. "Wait", said Marianne. The other nurse had joined her side. She ran up to them and took Kelso's arm as if to stop him but slid her hands down to his wrist and stretched his medical bracelet with much effort off his wrist. "I may have not told you the quickest way. You may want to go in the other direction down those elevators to the cafeteria. They may close the door if the cafeteria is at full capacity, so you should hurry." She put the bracelet in the pocket.

Guards spilled onto the third floor from the guest elevators.

"We'll take our chances. We may want to walk the hallways of the hospital and exercise our legs. Thank you," said Tom.

Kelso started to feel better. The other nurse shook her head and decided to head to the cafeteria herself.

Marianne went back to the nurses' station. She saw Dr. Edge standing there talking to an officer and federal agent. She knew what she had was golden, but she didn't know what to do with it. She needed a sympathizer, and Dr. Edge was busy. The head nurse was watching her closely.

Officers and agents were moving quickly; they were checking different hospital rooms and restrooms. Marianne made a face again, this time to Nurse Poohe. Nurse Poohe nodded her head. She made a face like she didn't feel well; she grabbed her bag and went to the restroom. She took her nurse's shirt off and switched it with another one she had in her bag along with a pair of pants. She was supposed to be off soon. So when she was caught. she hoped she would not lose her job.

She'd just purchased the shirt and pants in the boutique in the lobby. The style of the outfit was a little trendier than she was used to, but she didn't mind the change. Also, it would be a while before she could traverse any shopping malls from what she had heard on the news— especially now that the hospital was on lockdown. She almost felt safer at the hospital than braving it on the outside.

Marianne wished she would have been able to make

it to the locker room without being noticed so she could switch out her white sneakers, but even if she could have, it would have taken too much time. She gave herself a pep talk as she walked into room 384. She knew eventually that someone would check that room again as they watched the security monitors on the sixth floor and scoured the third floor for Kelso. The only person who had seen her walk into that room was Nurse Poohe.

Marianne lay down in the bed and pulled the sheets up past her waist. She took a pillow and put it over her head. She took the bracelet out and slipped it on her wrist. She left her arm hanging out on top of the sheets. She heard the doorknob turn. "He's here," yelled the guard.

Marianne made a deep moaning sound. Check his ID bracelet.

"Yeah, it's him," said the agent.

Nurse Poohe stormed into the room, pushed the agent aside, and picked up and looked at the wrist of Marianne, which now had a hospital band around it. She rolled her eyes.

Marianne made another baritone moan. "You need to leave this patient alone," Nurse Poohe said.

The agent who had put the hospital on lockdown stood in the doorway. He picked up his walkie-talkie, pushed the red button again, and said, "Code red averted. Stand down."

Nurse Poohe again turned to see the physicians and other attendants who were multiplying at the doorway. "This man has been heavily sedated. Everyone needs to leave now." She realized that his chart was still at the front desk with Dr. Edge and that she had made a mistake by drawing attention to the medication. "Dr. Keller must still have his chart," she said, hoping no one would notice the lack of protocol.

The actual chart was sitting on the front desk with Dr. Edge, who had gathered it back up to look over some of his notes.

Dr. Keller came to the room. "Great, he came to his senses. He was in no condition to be released," he said, smiling. "Where is his friend?"

He then went to the patient and looked at the thin wrist and the hospital bracelet. He read the name Kelso Brandon and then looked again at the thin wrist and pulled the pillow off of Marianne's head. "What the?" asked said Dr. Keller.

Tom and Kelso rounded the corner when they saw two young police officers coming their way. They waited for the officers to make their move, but the officers, one almost bumping into Tom, passed by them. They heard one officer say to the other officer that he had never tried to leave the hospital, and it was the doctor who was trying to force him to leave, but he was too medicated to go anywhere. The officers laughed at the inefficiency of the system.

Tom and Kelso exchanged looks. The hospital was still on lockdown, and they still needed to find a way out of the building without being stopped.

They found the elevator that was also the elevator for construction of the new wing. They entered the elevator with three other people. Tom had memorized the code

Dr. Edge had given him. He entered it into the keypad, and the door on the other side of the elevator opened. People looked out and smelled the fresh air as the door closed, and the two men disappeared before them.

Tom and Kelso walked out onto fresh construction. They had to find the stairs quickly—if there were any. They found some rope and tied it around their respective waists and hoisted themselves down to the next level.

"How are you feeling, champ?" asked Tom.

Kelso was not feeling any pain. The pill Tom had saved for him had done the trick. Kelso gave him the thumbs-up. They again hoisted themselves down another level and were able to make it out.

To distance themselves from others, they cut through the back lot and into the adjacent parking lot of the business park beside the hospital instead of going around to the front of the building. They didn't look back, but continued to walk, hearing yells and screams of people who were wanting to get into the hospital and others who wanted people to come out of the hospital.

Tom's eyes filled with tears, but they just kept walking. They went three blocks down and turned left. He was glad he had parked five blocks away. Any closer could have ended in trouble; they could have been spotted, or they could have been engulfed by all the other people. He still wasn't sure if the car would be there, considering the current events. He was grateful when he saw the car parked in the same spot.

Tom and Kelso were glad to be on their way home but wondered if it was safe to be going home. Kelso was white as a ghost.

Jasmine made it home to find Samuel texting his mother and Penny doing dishes in the kitchen. Beverly and Jag were sitting in the kitchen eating more breakfast. Penny had added fruit, cheese, and eggs to her already made breakfast, which included her blueberry coffee cake. She must have added a brown sugar crumble while or after it finished cooking since it looked more like a coffee crumb cake, she thought. *Apparently, Penny cooks when she gets anxious*, Jasmine thought to herself. "Looks good", Jasmine said, although, after where she had been, she had no appetite.

Silver jumped up. "No, Silver, down; stay down. You have to stay down. Can you grab him by his collar?" Jasmine said, addressing Beverly and Jag. "Also don't touch anything I've touched, like the front doorknob. I looked in on the Kilkennys."

Penny immediately left the kitchen dishes and met Jasmine in the hallway. "I thought you went for a run. You actually went to the Kilkennys'?" Penny paused to give Jasmine a chance to respond, but then continued. "Didn't you get the text from Tom? He copied me on it. The first text was that we were to keep Beverly and Jag here. The second was that you were to stay here and not go to the Kilkennys' house," said Penny, a little exasperated.

Beverly and Jag turned around to listen.

Jag and Beverly smiled as they waited for their answer. They were sure they were the only ones who cared about the Kilkennys. "Are the Kilkennys well?" Jag asked. He was turned around and was leaning on his chair.

"Darned if any of us are well," said Jasmine, thinking about her level of contamination, but she then thought again about the sensitivity of the situation. "No, they're not. I'm sorry. I'll explain after I finish with what I've started."

Jag and Beverly turned back around in their chairs. Jag put his hand over Beverly's hand on top of the table and squeezed. Beverly's eyes filled with tears.

Jasmine wanted more answers as to what this virus did and how contagious it was. "Has your sister texted you anything more about the virus?" Jasmine again wished she had bit her lip, as Penny was worried the most for her husband.

Jasmine told herself to focus on the task at hand. "Penny, please get me a garbage bag," she commanded.

And Penny obeyed.

Jasmine asked Penny to open the front door and throw out some soap, a towel, shampoo, and maybe some conditioner. As Penny opened the door Jasmine slid out to the front lawn. "Also, could you go and get some fresh clothes from my bedroom and toss them into the bushes on the front lawn?" Jasmine yelled.

Penny was once again obedient to Jasmine's request.

Jasmine stripped down in the front yard and bathed herself with the front hose and behind the bushes. She was glad Penny's home was such a private property. After she was finished, she put her clothes into the garbage bag and tied it into a knot. She left it by the side of the house. She then put her new clothes on and asked to be let back into the house. She was freezing cold, but she told herself that it would help her to stay on task. She took the only antiseptic wipes Penny had and wiped down the doorknob and washed her hands afterward.

"I'm freezing," said Jasmine.

Penny went and retrieved a throw from the top shelf of the front closet.

"Thanks, Penny," said Jasmine as Penny wrapped the throw around her shoulders. "I have another odd request, but it is just as important. Do you have a computer I could use and maybe discard after using it? It could be an old desktop or, well, anything old; and I'll reimburse you for it later."

Penny just looked at her. Reluctantly, she finally answered Jasmine. "I guess you can use mine, but I need to back it up to our online service first. You don't have to pay me back. If I were to guess, it's for the betterment of our current situation. I hope."

Jasmine looked at her and smiled. "Sorry, Pens, there's no time. But I know that I owe you an explanation," she said.

Penny retrieved her laptop from her bedroom. It was not as old as True Blue, but it was old, and she would not mind getting a new one. Almost everything she owned had sentimental value, which included her laptop. Even so, Penny was not unwilling to part with it for the right cause. She hoped this was the right cause.

Penny was regular on her backups, so she knew it should take less than two minutes to save any recent changes she had made to her hard drive. She opened her dual-core laptop and launched her backup utility application. *There, that should do it. How is that for efficiency?* Penny thought to herself. She looked at her watch, and the process was finished in under two minutes. The thought was directed toward Jasmine's odd but task-driven behavior.

Jasmine reminded Penny of her sister. Both were always up to something and never fully explaining themselves. There was never an explanation for what they were doing or why, but the results were always something astounding. Humm, Penny wondered.

Nancy once rewired the sound system at school so you could hear the principal reprimand a student, Nancy's nemesis, over the intercom. The student expected that Nancy had something to do with his embarrassing, all-to-public lecture from the principal but could not prove it. By the time the school secretary figured out what was going on, it was too late. The principal had already sentenced the student to detention, with the entire student body snickering at every word.

Nancy, out of the two of them, was the one who was always in control and knew what to do. Although Penny did not know Jasmine that well, it seemed like her friend and her sister's personalities were very similar. Penny was hoping that Jasmine would be able to spare some time shortly for her, Beverly, and Jag, so they also could be up to speed with what was going on in their neighborhood. Penny walked out into the living room and handed Jasmine her laptop.

Jasmine opened the laptop and inserted a Wi-Fi card. It was new technology in that it had its own MAC address and masked the MAC address of the computer she was using.

It had a pseudo IP address of four zeros separated by dots. It also piggybacked on other people's locked wi-fi within a 100-mile radius. "Great signal," she mumbled to herself.

Jasmine logged onto some anonymous text site and sent John a message to his phone. "John, I hope you and your friend are OK. I don't know much about the virus. But as you saw in the Kilkennys' dog and perhaps the Kilkennys themselves, the virus is fatal.

"What I know is that we're dealing with something that's very contagious. Hospitals are going on lockdown because of this epidemic. As for now, we believe the contagion may be bacterial. So burn everything you touched, no exaggeration. Try not to breath anything else in and be safe. If it's viral, what's needed is to just stay clean. Do both to be on the safe side. Don't go looking for any vagrants, who were friends of the Kilkennys and may be wandering the neighborhood. The initial phone call to the commissioner that you were kind enough to pursue was to report the Kilkennys' friends, who must have contracted the virus. I will only be at this text address for another two minutes. If you need to ask me anything, you need to do so now. Go." Jasmine pressed send

A minute and a half passed. Jasmine was looking at satellite feeds and had just picked one that was local to their vicinity when a text came in. "Jack is sick. We need help. Keep in touch, Jasmine, please." The text ended.

The concern on their end and hers was overwhelming. *Darn, can't anything be easy?* Jasmine offered up a prayer of thanks despite her concerns since she knew He was ultimately in charge. His presence was not always felt but known, God loves people.

The variables were unknown. "I will. I'll make some calls. Charge your phone and stay sterile and away from people. Treat Jack like he has a flu and try not to contaminate yourself. If there is a hospital that can take him in if he needs immediate medical attention tell them to send an ambulance. Let them know Jack may be highly contagious beforehand. Bye.", said Jasmine.

Jasmine finished perusing the local satellite feed. She knew there was one more thing she had to do before she logged off and dismantled. "OK, news text feed ... Here I go," said Jasmine as her fingers typed away. "Let the news fly." Jasmine typed some more.

She had always been against net neutrality, and there were a couple ways she would be able to attack it. She knew she had to act swiftly so bypassed the internet service providers, went to one of the internet sources, and wrote some code that would eventually be disseminated, which technically was not breaking the law. Some media feeds started to bottleneck, but her job was done. The news started to flow freely.

Jasmine thought of Jack and John. She hated getting involved on a personal level, but by grace she hoped she could handle it. She wished she had not gone to the Kilkennys. If it wasn't for Tom's suggestion, she would have stayed out of it.

Jasmine pulled up her messages and targeted the forwarded message from Penny. She pulled up Nancy's phone number and added it to her contacts. She called Nancy and left a message. She then texted Nancy from the computer. She typed, "I need some intel. I can call you on a secure line if you would like." That was her way of telling Nancy that they may be on the same clearance level.

Jasmine got up from her computer, walked into the other room, and smiled at Samuel as he looked up. "Are you having fun?" asked Jasmine.

Samuel nodded. He then added, "I will have much more fun when Uncle Kelso gets home, but thank you for asking."

She smiled again at Samuel and walked back into the other room.

Jasmine then sat back down at the computer and wrote the last text before she disassembled the computer and saved the hard drive for Penny. Everything Jasmine had done was from the terminal, so nothing should be able to be traced back to the hard drive.

Jasmine's last text was to Nancy. It read, "This is just an update for Mom. Samuel is playing on his phone and is waiting for Kelso to come home. Everyone is healthy."

Jasmine and Tom had been trying to conceive children for the last few years, unsuccessfully. She was happy for Nancy that she had Samuel.

Tom sent Jasmine a message saying they were finally headed home. *Perfect timing*, Jasmine thought to herself. "And Kelso is on his way home," she added to her text to Nancy. She pressed send. She then took a small adjustable torque screwdriver out of her clutch, pulled off the back of Penny's computer, and took out the hard drive.

Penny passed Jasmine as she was heading to her bedroom. Jasmine held up her hard drive, happy to have salvaged her computer, which, at some point, she should be able to use again. Penny put up her hand as if to say talk to the hand. "I don't want to know," she said and pointed to the three monkeys that sat on the mantel of their fireplace. I speak no evil, I hear no evil, and I see no evil.

Jasmine laughed. Penny trusted her instincts and realized that Jasmine was a lot like Nancy, certainly not perfect but not weak. Whatever Jasmine had gotten herself into, she would be fine with help from God above. How she wished she could believe, but there was so much she would never understand.

Tom looked over at Kelso and started to rethink every move he had made. "Kelso, tell me about how you're feeling?" he asked. If he had left Kelso at the hospital with the doctors, at least he would be treated. But his gut told him that they had made the right decision by getting out of that place.

Kelso, who was leaning back on the headrest, lifted his head. "I'm not sure if we should go home. You can drop me off at a hotel or, better yet, a motel and go to our house. Don't tell Penny where I am."

Tom turned to Kelso. "That's not the plan. We'll figure this out. I'm probably better off sticking with you. If you have it, then I have probably caught it already. By the way, Dr. Edge slipped these bottles into my jacket pocket. Or, I should say, I'm not sure how they could have gotten in my pocket other than Nurse Bratchet, but they're prescribed by Dr. Edge," he said, obviously was thinking out loud.

"Yes, it had to have been Nurse Bratchet. She must

have done it when the head nurse came into the room. She must have done it for Dr. Edge. Those are some smart sons of guns working at that hospital. It's the same antibiotic they were feeding you intravenously. It looks like it's at least a ninety-day supply. Wonder why so much." He handed it to Kelso and continued to drive.

Kelso read the note that was handwritten over the type on the subscription bottle. "Take a pill per day for at least ten days. This is a large dose of penicillin," said Kelso. Kelso noted that the prescription did not have his name on it. It must have come directly from the hospital medical supply. "Apparently,'', said Kelso as he continued to read the doctor's handwriting, "this works on the specific bacteria in question, and other antibiotics would not. Also, you're not contagious after twenty-four hours." Kelso looked forward to feeling better. He took a pill and closed his eyes.

Tom said a thankful prayer as he had been feeling guilty for smuggling Kelso out of the hospital in his ghostly condition but grateful they were free. "He wrote that all on the bottle?" asked Tom.

"No," Kelso said. "It was on a sticky note attached to the bottle. I still think we need to separate from the others until morning. That means I'll have been on the antibiotics for more than twenty-four hours and stand a lesser chance of being contagious if it's just bacterial."

Tom agreed. He pulled into a rundown motel at the edge of town but pulled back out.

"What are you doing?" asked Kelso.

"What if we go to Beverly's and Jag's house since they will be staying with Penny and Jasmine tonight?" Tom suggested. "I would have to tell Jasmine so she could make sure that Jag and Beverly didn't come home. Would you want me to tell Penny?" asked Tom.

Kelso had his eyes closed. "I'm not sure. We need to include Penny. I'll call her now," said Kelso, not quite up to a conversation but trying to keep his focus. "Hi Penny, how is my most excellent wife?"

"Better now," she said as she sat at the edge of her bed. "Are you on your way home?"

"Almost, I might be sick. I mean really sick. We need to hide out for about twenty-four hours. I just need to take some precautions before I come home. If your sister finds out anything else about this virus/bug, I really need to know."

"I don't want us to be separated. We will get through this together," pleaded Penny.

"Penny, if it was just you, then I might think about it, but it isn't. It's Samuel, too, as well as everyone else. I can't risk spreading this around. We were thinking we could stay at Jag and Beverly's; that way, we won't be too far away. What do you think?"

"I don't like being divided, and that's how I feel without you. But you're doing what's right. I'll tell Jasmine. She might be joining you.

"What do you mean? Jasmine is sick?" asked Kelso.

"No, no. Let her tell Tom. She went for a run this morning and she was pretty freaked out when she got back. She said she went to the Kilkennys, but she's been so busy since she came back that she hasn't been able to talk with me. I think they're dead," said Penny.

"We're turning onto Bakersfield. I'll have Tom call

Jasmine as soon as we get to Beverly and Jag's. Make sure they stay with you tonight. Remember, we are not divided; we are in it together. We are married until death does us part," Kelso regretted saying the death part as soon as the word came out of his mouth. "Love you, Money."

"Love you too!" said Penny, wiping a tear from her right cheek.

# Chapter 10

# Mom's House

Penny got up from the side of the bed and went to the bathroom. She shut the door. She leaned over the toilet and threw up. She knew it was nerves but convinced herself that she was just as sick as her husband. "Whatever Kelso has, I am sure I have," Penny said out loud. She was secretly OK with the notion.

Now if she could only convince Kelso that she was not well and she needed to recover with him. After all, he was only up the street. She knew he would never go for it, and she would probably have to wait it out. She rinsed her mouth out with water and dried her face with a towel and went to fix herself something bland to eat.

Penny took out the toaster and stuck some bread in it. She noticed Jasmine and Samuel playing on the floor. They were playing a game of Parcheesi. Jasmine was laughing, but she also looked preoccupied. Jasmine looked up and saw Penny. "You look a little green around the gills. Are you OK?" she asked.

Penny smiled. She realized there was not much that Jasmine didn't pick up on. "I'm doing all right, feeling a little queasy. I get that way when I get extra anxious. We need to update each other when I'm done eating my toast." said Penny.

She was glad to have Jasmine as a friend, even though sometimes she got on her nerves—or as of recent. Jasmine's matter-of-fact personality and Penny's bull-in-a-China-shop personality went well together on most occasions. They also had a lot of the same interests; they both like to be outdoors and do things, loved their family and husbands, avoided the fast lane, and were not workaholics.

Jasmine was actually on a sabbatical. Penny tried to remember what Jasmine did for a living, but it eluded her. They were both rather tall and fun to be around but had very somber personalities when it came to anything of significance. Penny again saw Jasmine as being like Nancy, whom she loved dearly, but sometimes could be overbearing and a bit full of herself. She was discovering there was a lot that she did not know about Jasmine, like she was handy with a screwdriver.

Jasmine continued to play Parcheesi with Samuel. "You should have eaten more breakfast this morning. That cake was some of the best I've had, and it was partially from a box. Who knew?" she said, setting a lighter tone.

Jasmine now addressed Samuel. "After we finish this game, I need to go and talk with your auntie." She once again turned her head toward Penny. "Have you heard from Nancy, yet he winked at Samuel. She was determined to win him over, but Sam was not an easy child to win over.

Samuel rolled the dice and looked down at his game pieces.

"Well it looks like you won. That was a good game. Beverly and Jag, do either of you want to take over?" Jasmine asked.

The couple had vacated the couch in the other room to join Jasmine and Samuel in the great room. They had made some personal phone calls from the living room but now were happy to have the fellowship of Jasmine and Samuel.

Jag, who was rereading a week-old newspaper, looked over the top of his paper at Jasmine and Samuel down on the floor. "I guess I'll give it a try, but it sounds like you are pretty good at this. You may have to refresh Grandpa's memory. I haven't played Parcheesi in some time," said Jag. Before Samuel could correct him, he added, "Not that I'm your grandfather, who I imagine you miss. But I have grandchildren of my own, and that's what they call me, Grandpa, among other things." A wave of emotion came over him. He missed his family, especially the grandkids.

Samuel's face brightened. "We could play a different game if you would like?" he said. "I like to play Travelers, Monopoly, Stratego, or Risk. Do you know how to play any of those games?" He felt much more at ease with Jag than he did with Jasmine.

Jasmine, tried not to have her feelings hurt. She grabbed her phone, which she'd had face up next to her while she was playing with Samuel, waiting for a phone call.

"Oh, thanks for playing with me, Jasmine," Samuel said coolly.

Jasmine turned around and gave him a slight smile as if to say, *I know that you know that I am trying too hard.*

Penny still looked a little green. She had finished her toast and put away the toaster. She was thinking of what she would fix everyone for lunch. Jasmine came and sat on the bar stool at the counter. Beverly came over and sat next to Jasmine on another bar stool. Jasmine put your hand on Beverly's hand and said, "I believe for right now this is a private discussion." She had already related her sympathy for the Kilkennys and had explained what she knew of the circumstances surrounding their death. She believed that their death was part of the epidemic.

Penny looked at Beverly and then at Jasmine. "She needs to be here. Beverly, you and Jack cannot go home tonight as you know. Tom and Kelso, who still needs to rest from his mononucleosis, is staying at your house," said Penny.

Jasmine had just been upped and she did not like it. Why had Tom not told her? She needed to be in the know at all times, but maybe not now; maybe that is who she used to be. She took a huge breath and then a couple additional small breaths. Penny looked at Jasmine, who had her eyes closed. Jasmine picked up her phone and texted Tom.

Jag looked up from his game to the conversation at hand. "Samuel, I have to take a break. I need to go talk with the grown-ups for a few minutes. OK, champ?" Jag said

Samuel understood but was disappointed. He looked up at Jag. "That's what my mother calls me," he said. He pulled his phone out of his pocket and went to find his charger. Jag went and stood behind Beverly who filled him in with details from their conversation.

Many questions still loomed. "Does this have anything to do with the Kilkennys? If Kelso is or has become infected with anything, we can't have them at our house,"

Jag said. "Jasmine, you said that the Kilkennys probably had that virus or infection or whatever it is. If that's right, then whatever is out there, anyone could catch. So if Kelso was at the hospital, he could be infected. Also, it's significant that those people are still at large somewhere out there. I don't know that Tom and Kelso will be safe with those vagrants at large. What if it was a murder not an epidemic that got the Kilkennys?" Jag looked around for Samuel to make sure he was not in earshot of their conversation.

Jasmine stayed composed. "That's the chance we have to take. We want to ensure Kelso is not contagious and Tom has already been exposed. They can also checkout to see if any of those stragglers who had singled out your house are still around. Tom will be able to secure your home, just in case."

Jag could tell Jasmine was one of those people who made sense no matter what she had to say.

Penny didn't have Jasmine's composure. She lost it. "Jasmine, you never told me exactly what you saw or where you were. You never told me how close you were to dead people. Are we in trouble?" she asked.

Samuel once again had situated himself on the floor with his phone plugged into the adapter next to him. Samuel looked up from where he was sitting.

"Samuel, would you mind going to your room?" Penny asked.

Samuel got up from his game and went to his room and shut his door. Jasmine looked down the hall to make sure he was in his room.

Everyone started talking at once. Jag put two fingers

to his mouth and whistled. Beverly picked up a pen that was lying next to a pad of paper on the counter and handed the pen to Jag. Jag rolled his eyes. "This is a talking stick," he said.

Jasmine giggled. Penny's jaw dropped. Beverly smiled smugly.

Jasmine turned to Beverly. "Let me guess. Former couple's counselor?" she asked. Jasmine started to develop an affinity toward Beverly and Jag.

Beverly smiled. "Yes, yes, I was for about thirty years. We are retired now. How did you know?" she asked.

Jasmine smiled and leaned closer into Beverly as if to tell her a secret. "Well, I would tell you. But I don't have the talking stick—or, in this case, the pen," she said Jasmine.

Penny finally smiled.

Beverly sat up straight and looked to Jag to ask the first question, but he just passed the pen to Jasmine, since her information on dead people trumped Penny's information on the whereabouts of Tom and Kelso. Jasmine was busy answering a text from Tom. She took the pen without looking up and said, "They are at your house. Do you keep a spare key anywhere? Or do they have to break in?"

"There's a turtle stone with a key in it in the backyard garden. It's hidden between the orange and apple tree," said Jag.

Jasmine typed the information into her phone. "OK, let's do this. This is what I know." Jasmine said. She was not going to go into all the details of everything she knew or had surmised. She needed to keep things simple. "The Kilkennys are dead. They were found locked in the bathroom. I'm not sure what their visitors had to do with that. As far as we could tell, it was some sort of disease that killed them."

The surprise was obvious. Penny's eyebrows were raised. "You said 'we' could tell." exclaimed Penny. "Who else are you working with?"

Beverly and Jag looked at each other. Then they all turned to Jasmine and stared blankly.

Jasmine was unfazed. "When I went to the Kilkennys, there were two cops who were investigating when they came across me. They were there as a result of Beverly and Jag's call to the precinct. They had thought it sounded suspicious and volunteered to investigate, even though they were not advised to do so. They came across a dog who was partly paralyzed from something, and then they found the Kilkenny couple. The assumption was made from the abnormality of muscles and skin condition that some sort of illness with which they were infected was the cause. It turns out that one of the cops from upstate New York, Jack, has become very sick as a result," said Jasmine. The thought of the dog made Jasmine vomit in her mouth. "Penny, do you mind getting me some water?"

Jasmine stared at her phone. She had texted Nancy over and over. She needed to hear from her as to any antidote or anything she could relay to the two policemen. Tom had texted Jasmine that Kelso was doing better and that the antibiotics were doing the trick. His skin color was coming back, and he didn't seem to be as warm as he had been.

"Thanks for the update," Jasmine texted back. She asked him how much of the antibiotics he had left.

He texted back that the doctor has given him over the amount he needed. He added that, even though Dr. Edge had written that Kelso should only have to continue to take a pill for another seven days, one per day, he'd been given a shot of antibiotics when they'd first arrived, and then there'd been the IV bag drip with penicillin. Kelso had already had a lot of penicillin running through his system.

"Kelso is doing better," Jasmine reported. She then tossed the pen over to Penny.

Penny didn't know how to guard a secret. "Kelso is not well enough to come here. It may be that bacterial infection. He and Tom are going to be staying at Jag and Beverly's house, since that's OK with you," she said.

Jag and Beverly were equally unpleased. "That's the plan. I guess I'll have to be OK with it. Whatever it is that is out there whether it is viral or bacterial I don't want our house to become contaminated." Jag said. "Can you tell me anything more about the bacterial part, Penny?"

Penny looked down. "No. I have yet to talk with Kelso at length. I think right now he just needs to rest, but Tom probably knows as much as he does. The rest I have to keep under my hat, as it is classified information," said Penny, not looking up from the counter.

Jag pounded his fist down on the counter. "Penny, I don't know how you came across your information. But we have a right to know. So does the American public. What's going on? We've been listening to the news, and we've heard nothing about an epidemic, but we have heard about hospitals being locked down."

Beverly now took the pen from Jag and put her arm on his to let him know not to lose his temper. "As of an hour ago, there are tons of tweets from all over the United States and some overseas US hospitals noting they've been put on lockdown," said Beverly. As she continued, she became a little confused. "The tweets just come across the top of my phone. I've been trying for the longest time to find a setting that will make it stop. But now I'm glad. I'm hearing and seeing things that our US news stations are holding back from us," she concluded proudly.

Jag did not bother to take back the pen but started to speak again. "Is this an epidemic? And do you know how widespread it is? The word *zombie* is coming up everywhere, and some people are taking advantage of the situation. We were not getting this information this morning or last night. We probably wouldn't have even come over here had we known how permeating this infection is."

Beverly inconspicuously slid the pen in front of Jag.

Penny did not bother to ask for the pen. "Taking advantage of the situation?" asked Penny. "I don't think so. You can't believe everything people tweet."

Jag wasn't ever sure about tweets. Jag looked down, embarrassed for his first time about maybe not having valid facts at his disposal. Beverly looked at Penny and gave her a look that said, *You should be ashamed.*

Penny smiled politely and left the table. "I'm going to fix some lunch," she said. Penny went to the refrigerator to pull out sandwich meat for sandwiches and some vegetables for a vegetable tray. She wasn't going to let Beverly shame her into being silent. But the more she was left alone to make lunch. the more she felt a little embarrassed.

Penny asked Jasmine if there was anything she wanted to add.

Jasmine said, "Not right now," which translated into, *We'll talk.* "I'm going to go for another run," she added.

Penny put her sandwich meat on the counter and faced Jasmine. "Oh no you don't. I know where you're going. I want to come, too."

Jasmine came close and tightly gripped Penny's arm and gave her a stern look. She pulled her from the kitchen into the mudroom. "If I don't go to Tom, then Tom has to come to me. If Tom comes to me, then Kelso will be left by himself. Do you want that?" she asked.

Penny looked perplexed. "What do you need from Tom that's that important?" She pulled her arm out of Jasmine's grip.

Jasmine wondered if she should answer Penny or not. "It's Kelso's medication. It should help save the cop from dying. At least it may help from everything I know about this infection. At the very least, it should slow it down."

Penny smiled at Jasmine as if she was not thinking correctly. "It's penicillin, Jasmine. It's been around for ages. You're going to tell me that that's the medication that's going to stop him from becoming infected or cure his infection?"

Jasmine saw Samuel come into the room. "It's worth a shot. It's a man's life. We have to try something," she said in a very low whisper. "Penny, I love you. I wouldn't do anything to jeopardize you or your family. I held my breath in case it was airborne when I went to see the dead dog. I never came near the Kilkennys bodies. I touched practically nothing but an outside doorknob. I showered and will burn my clothes later when I think it's safe to do so. I'm not taking you along because you need to stay safe, and I know how to stay safe. I know how to defend myself and others. By the way, I need the gun, just in case." Jasmine put her hands on Penny's face. "You feel warm, child. Do you have a thermometer? We need to take your temperature?"

Penny was a little more at ease. "I am feeling all right. I just need to eat something more than toast. By the way, Nancy texted me. She is really concerned about all your texts. Nancy said your proposed situation is exaggerated. Also, you don't have the same clearance level as she does because she is beyond clearance levels at this point. I think she was just teasing you, but I don't get it. She said you have nothing to worry about since I told her that Kelso was fine. She said not to text her anymore but to thank you for looking out for Sam."

Jasmine was morose. She was not used to being dismissed. "Hmm," she said. *Deep breaths*, she told herself. "Man, do I want to kick some butt," she said under her breath. "Need to go. Hold down the fort." Jasmine had to do one thing before she left. She did not have time to assemble and disassemble another computer. "Hey, Samuel, can I borrow your phone for one minute?" she asked.

Samuel looked at her and shook his head. "I don't think my mom would want me to lend it to you," he said. "Don't you have your own phone you can use? You need to keep it charged."

*This kid really does not like me*, Jasmine thought to herself. "I'll tell you what; you let me use your phone for right now, and I will make a couple of phone calls and then I will play any game you would like to play later when I get back," she said.

Samuel looked up at her. "Can I come with you?" he asked. "I am really bored, and I will be very good. I need some fresh air. My mom always tells me that."

"I wish I could take you. I would love the company. But right now is not a good time. I'm going to go meet your Uncle Kelso and my husband, Tom. I need to get something from them so we can help some other people out who need our help. So I'm going to do this quickly, and then I'll come back. And then maybe you and I can go out in the front yard and throw a ball if it's safe," she said.

"Tell Kelso that his nephew said hi. He will know who. It sounds like an important mission," Samuel said, now really wanting to go. He lifted his cell phone.

Jasmine placed her hand on the top of his head. She then took the phone from Samuel's hand and proceeded to call John, but John did not pick up.

That is strange. She then texted John, letting him know that she had medication for Jack. She so wished she had gotten his address from him.

"Hey, Little Trooper, would it be okay with you if I hung onto this phone for little while? Maybe until I see your uncle Kelso and return it to you when I get back?" she asked.

Samuel looked troubled. "My mother would not like that. She would be really angry. I think you had better give my phone back to me," said Samuel.

Penny walked over to Samuel and smiled. She handed

him a plate full of food. "I think just this once it'll be OK. Don't you?" she asked.

Samuel examined his food. The sandwich was cut into little smiling faces, next to the sweet potato fries that looked like swords, which, of course, only a young boy would notice. The watermelon was just cut into regular triangles but was his favorite fruit. He looked up at his Aunt Penny and said it would be all right just this once.

Jasmine stuck the phone in her pocket and went to get the gun from the shelf in the closet. She put the gun in the back of her pants. She knew this was a good time to ask God for some help. *Penicillin, what are the odds?* she thought to herself.

She offered up another prayer for the well-being of the two police officers, as well as Kelso and those surrounding her and a prayer for herself. "Lord, please let me do your will and not my will. Help me out with this. And thank You for helping others who need You too," she said.

She didn't change into her running clothes. Rather, just slid her running shoes onto her feet and laced up.

Tom texted Jasmine that it would be all right for her to come over. He wanted to find out more about what Jasmine had found out at the Kilkennys and couldn't wait to see her. They enjoyed their time and space apart from each other, but they liked their time together even better.

Kelso was sleeping on Beverly and Jag's couch. Tom decided to explore the house before Jasmine got there, which he'd briefly done when they'd first arrived.

"Beverly, Beverly," said a voice from behind the

couch in an incoherent mumble. Kelso was dreaming of rats scratching in the walls. "Bev— Beverly." Again came the words from behind him. There were more scratching noises. Kelso turned over. He saw someone in his dream who kept telling him to get up.

The figure behind the couch tried to pull himself up but collapsed. There was a thump on the ground.

Tom flew downstairs, skipping three of the last six stairs. He went to the man who was caught behind the couch, pulled him up by one arm, and looked into his face. He had almost luminous skin and deep dark circles around his eyes. He looked much worse than Kelso.

Kelso woke to see a gnarly hand resting on the couch and Tom standing partly behind the couch holding the man's other arm. He let out a yelp and grabbed his pillow and leaped to the other side of the couch.

Tom looked at Kelso's in disbelief. "How could you sleep through that?"

Tom was still holding the man's arm when the man tried to knock him over with his body. Then the man came at Tom with his face and tried to bite him. "What the heck?" said Tom, blocking the man from coming any closer to him with his forearm. Had the man not been in such an awkward position or so feeble, he might've succeeded in biting him.

Tom, who had his right fist free, slugged him in the jaw. The figure began to fall to the ground. Tom found himself still holding onto the intruder's arm. As Tom let go of the arm, he noticed much of the skin and flesh was still left in his hand.

Tom now was truly horrified. He looked at what he

was holding, an actual part of the intruder's arm, and quickly flung it across the room. It stuck to the wall by the door. Tom started to dance around and shake his hands, hokeypokey style. He kept repeating to himself the same question. "What the heck? What the heck?" He looked down at the person on the floor trying to crawl farther behind the couch.

Kelso had now jumped off the couch and was staring at the splattered remains of the man's arm on the wall. Kelso immediately felt sick with all the excitement.

"Keep an eye on him," Tom said as he headed toward the half bath off of the kitchen.

Jasmine knocked on the front door and tried to let herself in. "Tom it's me," she said.

Tom had not quite made it to the restroom to clean himself up. He looked at his hand and the wall. He nodded to Kelso to open the door. The man behind the couch moaned. Two police officers stood behind her. "Are you going to let us in?" she said in a jovial voice.

Tom put his hand behind his back. Jasmine, John, and Jack entered the house. Kelso just stood there with his mouth open.

"This must be Kelso, the sick one," said John.

Jasmine took Kelso's hand, which was trembling. Tom looked as bad as Kelso and was also visible shaken. Again, there was a moan behind the couch.

Jack and John surveyed their surroundings. John noticed the blood and flesh dripping from the wall. His hairs started to stand on end. "What's going on here?" he said as he drew a pistol from his side.

Jasmine went to Tom's side to see what was behind

Tom's back and heard John draw his weapon. She immediately stood in front of Tom and thought about drawing her gun, but a calm peace came over her.

Jasmine looked to her left and noticed the man behind the sofa. "Don't do that, John. There's a reason." She grabbed the couch, which was still at a forty-five-degree angle to the wall, and pulled it away from the wall, making it flush. The man reversed his crawl and came toward Jasmine and Tom. Jasmine and Tom lunged backward. Jasmine moved quickly for fear of infection, while Tom was still grossed out by the modern-day zombie. They stood together at the furthest corner of the room.

John now pointed his gun at the crawler. Jasmine drew her gun and pointed it at John. John now pointed his gun at Jasmine and then at the crawler and then back at Jasmine, tilting his head with confusion. As the man tried to get up, Tom moved closer to the crawler and placed his foot on his back, still not revealing what was in his hand.

"OK, does somebody want to tell me what's going on?" John said, not sure what to do with his gun.

Jack grew weak and sank to his knees. John put his gun back into his holster and picked up his friend with both arms. "A little help," he said as he started to drag him to the couch.

Kelso grabbed him and pulled him onto the chair. "Not the couch. There are human remains all over it," said Kelso.

Kelso went the bathroom and washed his hands. Jasmine took Tom's spot and lay her running shoe in the middle of the man's back as Tom followed Kelso into the bathroom and opened the trash bin underneath the sink and put what was in his hands in the trash.

"Do you mind standing a little further away from me?" asked Kelso.

Tom moved away from him, still totally disgusted.

Kelso finished washing his hands and moved to the side. "Which pocket is my prescription in?" he asked.

Tom leaned his right hip forward. Kelso reached into the pocket and pulled out his prescription. He then turned and poured soap over the prescription bottle and rewashed his hands. "Your turn," he said.

Kelso returned to the living room to find Jasmine and John hovering over the man on the floor. Jack was still in the chair. Kelso gave two of his pills to John to give to Jack. He then knelt next to the man on the floor and put two pills in his mouth.

"Thank you", said the man on the floor.

Kelso wasn't sure that the man would be able to swallow the pills. "We need to get him to his feet," said Kelso.

Jasmine and Kelso each grabbed one side of his body and pulled him up to his feet. They hoped that nothing else would fall off of him.

Jasmine tried to lean him against the wall. "Tom, grab us a glass of water," she said.

Tom surfaced from the kitchen with a small glass of water in hand. They tried to get the man to drink the water, but he was reluctant. In his bewilderment he grunted, "Not poison?"

Tom now had his hand against his chest. "No old man, not poison," he said.

Kelso left Jasmine and Tom holding the man. He found some antiseptic wipes under the counter in the kitchen and wiped off the couch. Jasmine and Tom gently placed their new friend on the couch, where he twitched and almost slid off.

Kelso looked at John, who stood once again on the other side of the room. He wasn't sure about the vibe he was getting from him. John seemed desperate. Kelso went back into the kitchen and poured some of the pills into his pocket. He poured another glass of water for John.

Jack had his eyes closed. "So what, this is what Jack would turn into if he continued to get sick? He would be like that dog he shot?" asked John. "How many pills do you have left anyway? You shouldn't give that guy anymore. It's not going to matter in the long run. I should shoot him to help him out of his misery. He's not even bleeding very much. Look at his wounds. There aren't not enough drugs for this guy and my buddy Jack. I have known Jack since grade school. We grew up together." As John spoke, he was growing more agitated.

Jasmine placed her hand on Tom's bicep. They were in agreement; they would cautiously wait to see how the situation with John would play out. It seemed as if he may be a little trigger-happy.

Kelso spoke as he walked past Jasmine and Tom. "I don't think this could've gotten any uglier, but it just did."

John asked him to speak up.

"This man's life has just as much value as anyone else in this room. No one but the Lord has the right to decide who gets to live and die. That's just wrong thinking. As

181

for his wounds, I've seen worse," said Kelso. He handed John the glass of water.

John grabbed the glass of water and thanked Kelso.

Kelso reached into his pocket and retrieved the half-empty prescription bottle of pills. "Here, have the rest of the bottle for you and your friend. You should take one, too."

John was a bit skeptical and wanted to make sure he had not been outsmarted. He opened up the top and took out one of the pills to make sure it was the same as what he had just received for Jack. He lifted the pill and popped it in his mouth and once again said, "Thank you." But this time he addresses his thanks to everyone.

Kelso approached Jack and knelt down beside him to look a little closer at his dilated pupils. "John, if you come down with anything, then you can get in touch with us. But try 9-1-1 first. That medication will have to take care of you both for right now. The dose I gave him was two pills. It's a jump-start. Hopefully, he'll be able to keep it down." As he spoke, Kelso only made eye contact with Jack.

Kelso noticed that Jack wasn't quite cognizant of what was going on around him. "It's what I had in the hospital initially. My dosage was in the form of an injection. Hopefully, I'm not poisoning him. That's also hoping that your friend isn't allergic," he added.

The conversation reminded him he needed to text Dr. Edge.

Kelso stood up and stared out the front window. He pulled out his phone and texted the doctor that he was doing OK and how his situation had evolved. He also mentioned Jack but let him know he hadn't caused Jack's infection.

The man with the gaping arm wound moaned that it would be all right if they let John shoot him. Jasmine went upstairs to see what she could find to bandage his wounds.

"More of my friends are coming," said the man on the couch, looking up at Tom.

Once again, John pulled out his gun and pointed it at the man. "The man wants to be put out of his misery," John said.

Jasmine came down the stairs with gauze, peroxide, and antibacterial salve. John was scared of Jasmine. He could tell she had a dark side, whether anyone would else could see it or not. He knew she would have shot him if he had come close to pulling that trigger. He was sure she was some sort of operative. He put his gun back down as she walked back over to the man on the couch.

Jasmine smiled at John in passing. "Not this again. Keep your gun in your pants. John, you're a good man," said Jasmine as she bent down next to the couch. "You went to check on the Kilkennys when no one else would. Don't let all this go to your head. Stay a good person; make good choices." She placed the peroxide on the man's arm. He winced.

Tom placed his hands on the man's shoulders. "Take your friend Jack and go where it's safe. Make sure you stay clean and burn or throw away any material that may have been contaminated. Make sure that Jack takes the medicine, a pill once a day." he instructed.

Jasmine, who now was applying the salve to the man's arm, smiled as she would have said the same thing.

Jasmine looked over to Kelso to make sure Tom had told him correctly. Kelso nodded his head.

"You can continue to text that number from which I texted you last. I will also text you with Kelso's doctor's information. He seems to be one smart guy to have figured part of this equation out. You will have Dr. Edge's information as soon as you leave." Jasmine had finished bandaging the man's arm.

The phone number was Samuel's. Jasmine knew she would be communicating back and forth on someone else's phone, but it was the only way she could stay in touch with John and Jack—people she did not 100 percent trust. In such precarious times, she barely trusted herself.

If she had to place bets, she would bet that Samuel's phone was a very secure and untraceable phone but government-issued; at least, that was what she had told Penny. Although it was not exactly a burner phone, it would not be trackable by the LAPD.

Jack opened his eyes and tried to get up but fell back down into the chair. "John, I think it's about time for us to go now—especially if they're expecting company," said Jack. "I wouldn't be much good in any sort of gunfight."

Jack took his gun out of his holster and flipped it around so the handle pointed at Kelso. Kelso took the gun and thanked him and put it in the back of his pants. Jack, once again, tried to get up out of the chair on his own. This time, he was successful. John let Jack lean on him.

"I am sorry for your misfortune," Jack said to the person on the couch.

"Thanks," John said as he turned to his small audience.

Jasmine watched from the front screen door as the

two officers made their way up the driveway. She listened for any complications but could hear none. She hoped their way home would be a smooth one. "How many pills do you have left?" asked Jasmine. "Can I have one, just in case. Tom, too? It may work as a preventative measure."

Kelso opened the other pill bottle and gave both of them a pill. He handed the second prescription container to Tom and asked him to hold onto it.

"If you take it for twenty-four hours, you're no longer contagious." Dr. Edge had texted Kelso back with more information. "Dr. Edge wrote that the infection is a variation of the bacteria, *Pestila sinera*, which caused one of the plagues."

Jasmine and Tom absorbed every word that Kelso read.

"It definitely works on the muscles and the flesh. The doctor says to continue to take a pill once a day, drink water, and get as much rest as possible." He felt his pocket full of pills. "We have enough right now for everyone. I am definitely feeling better, other than my spleen, which is still tender. I do need rest and maybe a shower. What I would not give for a clean change of clothes and to sleep in my own bed next to my perfect wife."

"We had better stay here until we're all clear of this contagion—twenty-four hours. You need to talk with Penny," said Jasmine. "I will start decontaminating, starting with this wall. Kelso, check under the sinks and cabinets for cleaning supplies, if you're up to it." She walked over to the wall, which had been the target of Tom's throwing. "Tom, start cleaning upstairs. Strip the beds and throw down the sheets. Look for any unusual streaks on the walls or anywhere else. Bacteria can spread through clothing as well air and other mediums." It was general information she was disseminating, but it helped if everyone was on the same page.

Nancy and a few other key officials huddled together behind a big mahogany table going over the intelligence they had been given. Nancy, a specialist in international relations and security, had many questions with regards to Iran's invasion of Iraq and their threats against the United States and Israel. She combed through the documents as soon as she was handed them.

Nancy was to meet first with the Secretary of Defense and then the chief of staff. She had to brief them both on what she and her team had surmised from the latest information. Unfortunately, she found the information to be anything but complete. She needed to see the image map of the invaded area. There needed to be pinpoints of exactly where the borders had been compromised, which, even with the satellite images, was still speculative. Much of Iran's invasion was covert. It was done through tunnels and crossing the border secretively.

The Iranian government had been infiltrating Iraq for years, even with the United States' military presence. It was easy enough since both Iran and Iraq spoke the same Arabic language. The military personnel did not distinguish between the inhabitants of Iraq and Iran, especially since the Iranians were trying to blend in. Besides, the military was there to keep peace, not to look for counterespionage.

To a trained eye, it was easy to see the differences and the pathways that were frequently being used to transport personnel and weapons. Advanced defense technology and other weapons were smuggled though tunnels and over the borders via urban and rural routes. It was Nancy's job to find the weakest links and shut them down.

The Iranian government choose to associate with different factions of antigovernment but pro-Arab alliance organizations for assistance. For whatever reasons, Al Qaeda was the exception and would not recognize the Iranian government. They leaked as much information through civilians as possible to the US military. They even had satellite images that outed some of the warehouses through which some of the tunnels existed. Also exposed by the satellite images was an old chemical warfare plant of mass destruction. *Bush Junior was right*, Nancy thought to herself.

Nancy held these photo images in her hand and simultaneously perused the satellite footage. The military experts had not seen the covert, invasive maneuver of the Iranian government coming, but the pictures screamed a thousand words to Nancy. She immediately noticed the not so subtle differences of the woman's clothing and the men's turbans. "How long has this been going on?" she asked Nancy. She looked for the earliest dates on the pictures.

General Ira, who had been sitting a couple of seats down from Nancy, grabbed the picture that Nancy laid on top of the other dozens of photos in the middle of the table and slid it in front of him. He looked closely at the warehouse and then at the people going into the warehouse. He also noticed the discrepancies.

Ms. Kane opened the door to the conference. She announced that Chief of Staff Denis McDonough could see them now, and the Secretary of Defense would join them shortly. Nancy felt like she had been caught with her pants down. Ira looked at Nancy and then at Ms. Kane and pushed his chair away from the table as he stood up. Nancy took two pictures from the table and added them to her collection of documents. The main points of the documents and photographs would be easy to speak to, and then the general could take it from there.

Nancy called. "How are you doing? How are *we* doing—'our country tis of thee'? Did you talk to the president?" Penny asked.

"I will brief you later, little sis. I need to get straight to the point. Can I talk with Samuel?"

Penny handed the phone to Samuel.

Samuel was excited that his mom was calling him. "How are you, Mom? Oh my phone?" said Samuel as he looked at his aunt. "Aunt Penny said it would be OK if Jasmine borrowed it. She will bring it back when she's done. No, I'm not sure when she's going to be back. She went to see Uncle Kelso, who is very sick, but should be back tomorrow."

Penny was reaching for the phone, but it was too late. The damage was done.

Samuel looked at Penny, not sure if he had said something wrong. "Yes, Mother, I know. But Aunt Penny said it would all right. She's right here. Penny, your sister wants to speak to you. She says I need to go pack my things. I don't want to go to Mom's house, our country cottage. I don't want to stay with Grandma and Grandpa. I want to stay with you and Uncle Kelso. Tell her that," said Samuel, covering the phone with his hand—something she was sure he had probably seen his mother do. "I hope Uncle Kelso feels better soon," he added as he handed phone back to Penny.

Penny smiled at Samuel and his big, compassionate heart. But as for her sister, she rolled her eyes and took the phone from Sam. "Are you coming to get Samuel? You don't have to do that; everything is under control. Kelso should be back tomorrow. He should not be contagious any longer," said Penny, continuing to be positive about Kelso's condition.

Penny watched as Samuel left the room to go pack for his mother. "As for Samuel's phone, it was a one-time deal. Jasmine needed to borrow Samuel's phone because she had to make an untraceable call. That's what she told me. She couldn't have whoever she was texting or calling be traced back to her phone."

Nancy was quiet. Penny knew that, if her sister was quiet, she was furious. "That doesn't make any sense. You let her have my son's phone so that it could be traced back to my son. That doesn't make any sense. Did she think my son had an untraceable phone? Because it's traceable. I know she's a mile and a half down the road from your house. I knew the minute she left the house. I could see her through the camera lenses, and then she stuck the darn thing in her pocket. I'm coming to pick Samuel up. And then I'm taking him to my house in Wyoming to stay with Mom and Dad. You should come too," said Nancy.

Penny was distraught. "You don't have to come pick him up. Kelso will be back tomorrow, and Sammy was really looking forward to hanging out with him. He won't be contagious anymore. Also, don't be mad at Jasmine and Tom; they have been a great help to us. We truly could not have survived without them."

Penny needed Nancy to reconsider, not that Jasmine and Nancy needed to be friends but just that Nancy would be comfortable with leaving Samuel with them. Penny tried to think of anything else she could say to get Jasmine off the hook. "I'm not sure why Jasmine had to borrow the phone from Samuel, but she took apart my computer when she wanted to communicate via text the first time. She is very capable." Penny was thinking out loud and could only hope that any additional information would help their cause.

Penny tried to remember what Jasmine had told her. "I think it had to do with the fact that she was texting a cop about an incident at one of our neighbors' houses. She knew that a police officer could trace the phone number back to her name and address, as opposed to Samuel's phone number, which, if registered, would have been out of state. She may have also been worried about the GPS thing, but she didn't say so."

There was thirty seconds of quiet. "Penny, let me bold and brief with you on what I know. The top leading doctors and scientists are still not sure what this contagion is. Just because the doctor gave Kelso a clean bill of health does not mean he's OK to be around—not that I believe he has anything more than mono and some sort of infection," Nancy said. She waited for Penny to say something, but Penny was still thinking about her husband.

"As far as your location, you're not as safe as I thought you would be. People in droves are vacating towns in hopes of finding some sort of safe haven, especially with this illness. Groups of individuals are looking for houses to inhabit. There's been more than one occasion where people have killed homeowners. Also, those who are sick are banding together. We are not sure where they're going or what they're doing, but they're vagrant as well." As Nancy spoke, she was walking onto her company's plane. Penny could hear the engine running in the background. "I will be there in less than five hours. This time, I will come to your house. Please, Penny, think about coming with us. I am bringing a doctor to examine Kelso."

Penny hung up the phone with Nancy. Jag and Beverly were on the couch listening to their conversation. "Nancy is right—if this isn't safe for Sam," Jag said. "If she can keep Samuel safe, she needs to do that. Beverly and I aren't sure about what we're going to do. We already had vagrants wandering around our back garden. Heck, they may be even in our house right now. That would be awful. Tom and Jasmine would have to fight them off. My money would be on Tom and Jasmine," he added.

Penny wasn't concerned about Beverly and Jag. She hadn't even thought about what they were going to do. She now recognized that they would need a place to stay. She could offer to ask Nancy when she arrived if they could go with them to Wyoming.

Penny went and sat next to Beverly on the couch. "I

need to ask you a favor. I will see if you and Beverly can stay with us in Wyoming, or at least we could provide you with safe transportation to somewhere. But what I need right now from you is to take care of Samuel and maybe let Silver outside. I need to go and see Kelso and let him know our current state of affairs," said Penny.

She waited for them to say something, but they just stared at her.

Penny looked at Samuel, who had obeyed his mother and finished packing his things. She again directed her attention to Jag and Beverly. "I want to see how he's doing with my own two eyes. Nancy will bring a doctor to examine him, but if he's not able to go with us, then they will have to leave us behind. But whether we stay or go, it should not affect you. I just need to see him," she said.

Jag and Beverly both were shaking their heads. "We don't think it's such a great idea," Jag said. "This could impact all of us. You really don't want whatever this 'bug' is. Hospitals are on lockdown. Some people say it's equal to the black plague. People are dying out there. Other people are just going crazy because of everything that's happening. This isn't something you want to mess around with when it comes to other people. I know how you feel about your husband, but you still need to be cautious."

Jag knew his words had no impact. Penny had made up her mind. He would try one more approach. "I would ask that of my Beverly and she would obey. Just as I know Kelso asked that of you," he said.

Beverly nodded in agreement.

Penny smiled. "I won't go inside the house. I will stay outside the house. I will not come in contact with Kelso,

Jasmine, or Tom—although I do believe that Kelso should not be contagious after twenty-four hours of taking this antibiotic. Do you know what that means?" Penny asked, not waiting for an answer. "As of this evening, no one will be able to catch this infection from him. I promise I won't be in physical contact, but I do need to go and see him. I hope you understand. You have Tom's phone number. Use it if anything comes up."

Jasmine was cleaning off the scattered remains left on the wall when she heard the knock on the door. "Kelso, Tom, Jasmine, it's me, Penny. Can I come in?", asked Penny. She knew what the answer was going to be and had not planned on coming in until she arrived at the door.

Kelso got up from the kitchen chair where he was resting. Jasmine stopped what she was doing and instantly stood up. She motioned Kelso not to come to the door and not to say anything.

"I was not planning on coming into the house unless you think it would be alright. I just need to see Kelso through the window. Or I can talk through the door." Penny said innocently.

Kelso walked over to the front window and looked out. Penny saw his face and smiled.

"I just need to tell you a few things." She mouthed the words through the window as if Kelso could read lips. "Open the window." She lifted her hands as if showing him how to open a window.

Kelso locked his eyes on Penny. Jasmine kept repeating

to him that she could not come in. He drew closer to the window and quickly opened it. Then his eyes became strained. It wasn't Penny he was looking at anymore. He was looking past her at something in the background, something that was moving closer to her. He pulled his gun from the back of his trousers and fired through the window screen.

Kelso wasn't shooting to kill. He was shooting to frighten the intruders. The sound of the gunshot did the trick. Two people came out from behind the trees moaning and hobbling.

Jasmine had already had the front door wide open and her gun pointed past Penny's head. "I have a clear shot," Jasmine said.

Tom bolted downstairs in time to hear Jasmine say she had a clear shot. He put his hand on her shoulder, not sure if Jasmine would shoot. He put his face close to her ear. "Stand down," he said.

Kelso looked at Jasmine as if she was from a different planet. She slowly pulled back her gun as she watched the intruders scramble in different directions. One went toward the driveway. The man on the couch started to moan again.

Penny jumped to the side and saw the vagrants go in opposite directions. She had sprinted forward into the bushes, confused by the gunshot and the vagrants. "Is anything ever going to be normal again?" she asked as she emerged from the bushes and picked a twig off her sweater.

Kelso and Tom now were headed toward the front door. Kelso moved closer into the door, but Jasmine put her hand out stopping him within a couple of feet. "Penny, you're a sight for sore eyes.", said Kelso.

Jasmine touched Kelso's chest. "I'm sorry you can't come in. But as you can see, it's not safe, either inside the house or outside," said Jasmine, trying to control the situation. "What are you doing here?" she asked.

Penny knew Jasmine was mad at her, but she didn't care. She looked at Kelso and took in every detail of his demeanor. Kelso pushed his way past Jasmine's hand.

Penny smiled that Kelso would not let anyone push her around. She thought she heard something and looked behind her but saw nothing. She decided to let the ones in front of her be her eyes. "Kelso, you look wonderful. You look much better than you did before you went to the hospital," she said. She was determined to have Kelso well, whether he was or not.

Kelso started to put his hand on the door latch but then stopped.

"Well, I guess I should make this quick," Penny said with a quiver in her voice. "Nancy is sending a doctor for you. She's also coming to pick up Samuel. She wants to take us back to Wyoming. We would be safe unless something falls on us from above. What would be the chances of another comet falling in the same state again? The super volcano in Yosemite could blow." She was desperately trying to lighten the mood. She let out a, "Ha," like it would be funny. She realized she was rambling. She continued. "But I think we will be safe, all of us. This area isn't safe according to Nancy, but we will be once we get to where we are going." Penny started to cry.

Kelso knew that look. Penny under stress became

very active with organizing and keeping busy. But after the busyness wore off, she would spiral down and become a little more pensive. Penny needed to be in control, but she wasn't.

Kelso wished he could comfort her, but he thanked God for Samuel. Samuel added another variable to Penny's personality. He could not put his finger on what it was, but it was the reason she did not come into the house. Kelso knew that, as long as Penny had Samuel, she would keep it together and would do her best to make everything work together for good.

Kelso was closest to the door as he spoke intimately with his wife. "Penny, I wish I could hold you right now. But I can't. I'm not sure that the doctor can agree to let me go with you. I'm still taking the medication, and I will probably get better. But this is still with me. I want you to be safe. Jasmine and Tom should go with the rest of you. I am pretty sure that the doctor will find them well enough to travel. Hopefully, the doctor will also be able to do something for the man on the couch. There must be some sort of safe haven for the sick."

Penny looked beyond Kelso to see if she could see the sick person on the couch. She saw a hand lift up off of the couch. She figured it was a symbolic of a wave. Penny was distraught. "That man is really, really sick. Whoever has been near that guy is probably not going to be able to travel," whispered Penny. Mostly likely, it would be all of them hanging back until everyone was well, she thought to herself.

Tom and Jasmine both shrugged their shoulders at the comment. It may be a possibility that the man on the couch could travel, but he was too ill to actually travel without a medic.

"Can you text Nancy that penicillin has been effective and, if they could get their hands on any penicillin for us, that would be a positive," said Kelso.

There was another moan from behind Kelso.

Penny wiped her eyes and twisted her head as if she was twice as confused. "This person, does he have a name? How sick is he? Is he definitely sick with what we have been hearing about on the news?"

Jasmine stepped forward and was by Kelso's side. "He is no one you need to worry about right now, Penny. It's a man who is definitely infected. His muscles have atrophied, and his skin tissue is too thin. We're not sure what we can do for him, but we are trying. We can't take him to get medical attention, so we're treating him the best we're able. Tom and I are both on antibiotics so that we will not be contagious, but we definitely have been exposed. I'm sorry. I wanted things to be much easier than this. I know how hard this is for you."

Penny hated every word out of Jasmine's mouth. She had no idea how hard this was for her. She got to be not only with her husband but also with Kelso. It was not fair. She wanted to be exposed, but she knew that would be beyond asinine. "I'm not leaving without you, Kelso. When Nancy comes, I'll bring her and the doctor back here. I'm going to walk home now," she said.

Kelso exchanged a glance with Tom. Tom nodded and took the gun from Kelso's hand. He grabbed an antiseptic wipe from Jasmine, who was dangling one from her fingers for Tom. Tom quickly wiped down the gun and dropped the wipe to the floor. "I will follow her at a distance and come back soon," he said.

Tom gave Jasmine a kiss as he headed out the door. Tom wondered if he was going to run into anymore of the vagrants or whether they had scared them off for tonight. He felt sorry for Penny but was happy for the hope she brought. *Wyoming*, he thought to himself.

# Chapter 11

## Saving Grace

Nancy showed up within the five-hour time frame as promised. She rolled up the driveway on a motor scooter. Samuel was the first to see her from the window. Aunt Penny held the door open as he ran to his mom with his arms wide open. Nancy had parked the motor scooter and disembarked. She now had her arms open wide too. Samuel jumped up into her arms.

"It's good to see you, champ," said Nancy and gave him a kiss. "Are you all packed?"

Samuel nodded. "Great! In that case, we should be on our way soon. And you are just a few short hours away from seeing your grandparents."

There was rumbling sound in the distance of another motorbike. Penny was walking slowly toward Nancy and Samuel as one more scooter started to make its way up the driveway. It pulled up next to Nancy's bike and parked.

Dr. Evo clumsily got off the scooter and made his way toward Nancy. It was plain to see that Dr. Evo was not comfortable riding on his motorbike; they watched as he pulled at his pant legs and wiped his brow with his pink polka dot handkerchief, a gift from his fiancée.

Samuel looked Dr. Evo up and down. He was not sure the doctor was good enough for his mother to date. The doctor was about the same height as his mother but not as old. "This is another one of your friends, Mom?" Samuel said in a very mature tone.

Nancy took the helmet she'd placed on the ground and put it on the handle of the bike. She gave Samuel a little tap on his shoulder and a somber look to let him know he should know better. "This is Dr. Evo. He's here for your Uncle Kelso; he's going to help him get better. He's also going to need to look at everyone here, including you. We don't have too much time. So we'd better get started."

As Nancy finished, the doctor bent down to look at Samuel. Crouched down to Samuel's level, Dr. Evo talked to Samuel the same as he would one of his patients back home. He explained everything he was doing. He looked in Samuel's eyes for proper dilation and tested his reflexes.

Nancy smiled as she laid her hand on Penny's arm, never taking her eyes off of her son and the doctor. "Hi, Penny. Sweetheart, it's so good to see you. Thanks for holding it together. I cannot imagine walking in your shoes." Nancy still did not make eye contact with her sister.

Jag and Beverly opened the front door to let Silver outside. They walked down the steps to the doctor and Nancy. Jag put out his hand. "Hi, I'm Jag. And this is my wife, Beverly. So you're, Nancy, the one who's going to save America. Very, very, glad to meet you." Jag held out his hand and waited for Nancy to return his gesture.

Nancy readily shook hands. The firmness of Jag's handshake made her look again at his face. "Save America perhaps, but mostly the United States. Congress?" Before he could answer, she added, "Yes, US Senate. I don't know why I didn't recognize you. My brain's a little cloudy with all the furor."

Jag smiled, along with his wife. They looked like they were greeting someone at an inaugural ball. "That's correct. I am partially retired now," he said.

Nancy then looked at Beverly. "And you are Beverly?" She, held out her hand.

Beverly had a firm handshake as well. Nancy was glad for Beverly's white eyes and the strength of her grip. She seemed healthy.

"It's always an honor to meet the wife of a former senator. I know how much you have done behind the scenes, and I am a fan," said Nancy. She was very familiar with political rhetoric and pleasantries. In politics, pleasantries were usually exchanged before anything of importance was said. Nancy found that there were very few political figures, except for the president, who came straight to the point. She was very thankful for the current president, who was not only straightforward but also unafraid to make the hard and unpopular decisions for the United States and abroad.

Most politicians had to use turns of phrase to get back to any topic of importance like, "Let me be candid," or, "I'll get straight to the point." Nancy herself stayed away from rhetoric in general—always had, even when she was younger and spent much of her time on the Hill as a lobbyist. Nancy stayed candid and only interested in the objective of her lobbying. She was younger then, no doctorate degrees, engaged to Samuel's father, and not a lot of fun to be around. She could hobnob with the best of them. But mostly, Nancy chose to keep to herself. She was on the "exclude list" for happy hour invitations or any other cordial invites, but why did she need them? She had her fiancé and her aspirations outside of the Hill. For Nancy, that stint had been only a stepping stone in the many steps of becoming who she was today.

Nancy was not addressing Jag and Beverly as retired politicians but was being personable. She was gracious to the people who, no doubt, had helped to look after her son in some way. Nancy was a straight shooter and chose her words wisely. She knew what Beverly and Jag wanted from her and had no problems offering it up, as long as they were healthy and were willing to contribute to the whole, which she knew they would.

Nancy looked back at the doctor. "Would you two like to stay with our family in Wyoming?" she asked. She petitioned for the doctor to come forward. "This is Dr. Evo. If the doctor says that the both of you are fine for traveling, then we would love to have you. We have plenty of room. It's a big house in the middle of nowhere and is a safe shelter. We are working to make it even more secure." Nancy paused and tried to read their blank faces.

"I have to be honest; this area has become highly volatile. It may not be safe for you here any longer," she added.

Jag nodded his head for the both of them. Jag and Beverly knew this would be a stepping stone to securing a safe place for their whole family, with whom they had been in constant contact.

"It will be a great honor to have you, but I would ask you to pitch in wherever you can," said Nancy.

Dr. Evo stepped forward.

The doctor quickly checked everyone. When it came to Penny, he took an extended amount of time testing her reflexes, looking into her eyes, checking her lymph nodes and just feeling for muscle. He looked at her as if he had something else to say to her, but he didn't say anything except that she was free to travel. He gave everyone a clean bill of health.

"I guess now we just have to go see those friends of yours and your husband, Kelso. Are we walking or driving?" asked the doctor.

Nancy pointed to Penny's car. "We should take the wagon," she said. "It seats at least seven. If we need another vehicle, when we get to Beverly and Jag's house, we can procure one. If anybody has anything they need to bring with them, bring it now. You have two minutes." She took a small satchel from the back of her bike and walked toward True Blue.

Nancy nodded at Samuel. Samuel went to get his bags and returned to the car. She opened the door to the back seat of the car and waited for Samuel to buckle himself in. Nancy took his bags and laid them at his feet. She threw her satchel in the back seat next to Samuel's bags. She then sat in the driver's seat and waited for Penny to give her the cars keys.

Penny was reluctant to let her sister drive. But what could her sister do to True Blue? It was indestructible. Still, she would hold on to the keys for a little longer.

It was now getting dark, and nobody had eaten dinner. Penny thought about what she should feed everyone. She would snatch a cooler, a couple loaves of bread, and sandwich meat. She would also take anything else from the refrigerator that was easily accessible. She put some things in a brown paper bag and others in the cooler.

Penny knew she could work within the two-minute time constraint. She started out the front door when she remembered her cross and quickly ran back to her room and grabbed it off of her dresser. She thought to grab St. Andrews from the windowsill but decided to leave it for the house. Penny went to Kelso's top dresser drawer and took out his Bible.

She had already packed for Kelso, and their bags were sitting on the front porch. She couldn't think of anything else that she needed. She grabbed her brown bag of groceries and cooler and went to the front porch. Jag and Beverly had already loaded Kelso and Penny's bags from the front porch into the car. Jag took the cooler from Penny's hand and escorted her to the car. She handed Nancy her car keys as she joined Nancy in the front seat. Silver was the last to jump into the car after doing his business and lay at Samuel's feet.

Jasmine was sitting next to the man moaning on the couch. She was tired of his lack of communication. She didn't know whether she should encourage him to walk around or not but was worried about his circulation.

Jasmine thought about aspirin. Her best guess without consulting his doctor was to give him a small amount, maybe 180 milligrams of aspirin on a daily basis. She and Tom made it their mission to research via their smartphones all tweets and news sources in relation to what may be helping the victims of the infection. Most of what they had found was bogus—herbal remedies that were questionable. But some things seemed to them could help with the slowing down of the symptoms, which were basic muscle atrophy and lack of circulation. The lack of circulation probably came first. Eventually, the nervous system was affected as different parts of the body started to shut down. The facts were few.

The man on the couch remained nameless. Jasmine had gathered bits and pieces of information from Jag and Beverly as well as John as to who the stranger on the couch might be. He had been undergoing a new cancer treatment which may have hastened the effects of the infection. They were limited on what they could and could not get their hands on, but aspirin they had. Jasmine gave him two aspirin to start out their theory.

Jasmine decided not to have him walk to increase his circulation. "What is your name?" asked Jasmine for what seemed to be the twelfth time. She didn't know if she could contract this infection by just sitting next to the man. But bacteria, she reasoned, could be transmitted through air, water, and material, so her chances were good for being infected.

The back of the couch seemed a good place to rest her arm. She wanted to hold him or his arm but did not. She did not know whether this would inflict pain or whether she just faced contaminating herself. Jasmine knew she couldn't just sit there. She at least needed to find out his name. Life was too short; to live one's life in fear was not to live life. Jasmine at least needed to know his name.

Tom warned her with his eyes to be careful. After all, the man had tried to bite him.

Tom joined his wife and the man but crouched down on the floor in front of Jasmine instead of sitting on the couch. "What's your name?" asked Tom.

The man could barely look at him. The man laid his head against the back of the couch. They asked him if it would be all right if they prayed over him. They interrupted his groan as a yes.

Tom placed his hand on the man's knee and prayed out loud. "Dearest Father, please heal this man amid these awful circumstances. Let him know Your truth and Your love for him. Amen," he said.

Amen followed from both of them. They were not sure what they would be able to do for the man, but each silently prayed that God would intervene and that His will would be done.

There was a knock on the door. Kelso got up from his chair. He ventured to the door to find Nancy, Penny, and the doctor standing there. Jag, Beverly, Samuel, and Silver were hidden in the back seat of True Blue. Nancy didn't ask if it was all right to be let in but rather just walked through the door, with Penny and the doctor following. Nancy pointed the doctor to the man who was on the couch.

The doctor stood over the man.

He lifted his head and said, "Campbell. My name is Campbell." It was the first time that he had remembered his name. He started to remember more than he cared for. "We are guests of the Kilkennys." His head was still not very coordinated, and his eyes dashed to-and-fro.

The doctor tried not to act surprised by Campbell's condition, but he was. So far, the very advanced stages of this contagion didn't allow for talking or any coordinated movement. "Campbell, you are one for the records. You are not well enough to travel with us but well enough to be treated in one of our government lab facilities. I can call and see where you will be accepted. Let me look at your arm."

The arm had been neatly bandaged. While Dr. Evo carefully unwrapped the gauze to look at the wound Jasmine filled him in on the information she had. He examined the arm and made a face. He noticed the abrasions around Campbell's mouth and other places on his body. "Hmm, his lack of immunity has opened up his system to other viruses, which may assist in spreading this bacterial infection so quickly. But these abrasions on his arm aren't from the flesh-eating bacteria. I'm not sure what happened to his flesh to make it so pliable that it could be easily severed. It seems people are being affected differently throughout different nations. Only a small percentage of bacteria is harmful, less than 5 percent." Dr. Evo was another doctor who could not keep his knowledge or thoughts to himself, but all who were listening were grateful.

Dr. Evo wrapped Campbell's arm again after applying a strong antibiotic salve. He also took a butterfly needle and withdrew a vessel of blood. He then injected Campbell with another antibiotic that worked with Penicillin—this one to treat his respiratory system. He put the blood in a battery-operated portable cooler he carried with him. The doctor decided to wait to give Campbell a pain reliever or something that would help him sleep.

Dr. Evo looked at Nancy, who had her phone to her ear. "We have to transport this man to somewhere safe, where he is not targeted by the populous as an infected. He has hope, but we cannot treat his cancer. Actually, his cancer treatment, in combination with the bacteria, could account for his lack of plasticity in his skin and the thinning of his epidermis; thus, his skin was able to come apart so easily. Hmm … fascinating. It was obvious, once again, that the doctor was talking to himself, and the rest of the group was just able to hear him.

Kelso stared at the doctor and wondered why doctors had such a special language of their own. "I'm not keeping up with the news," Kelso said prefacing his next question. "What happens if he's left alone? How would he be targeted as an infected by the populous?"

Dr. Evo looked at all of them gravely. "This is the part that won't be reported by the news, but it's making the Twitter feeds. People are eliminating those they believe to be infected on site. It's gruesome. People have seen far too many zombie movies. These people are not the undead. They are the other definition of zombie, a person who mechanically is unable to control his apertures. They are lifeless, apathetic, and not always lucid." Dr. Evo was one of the more compassionate doctors. They had sourced information that other doctors been more indifferent to those who had been infected. They were being isolated verses treated. "Kelso, you said you've been treating him with Penicillin. Was there anything else that he has been treated with?" The doctor targeted Kelso with the question to test his level of focus.

Kelso had this, but all of a sudden, he wasn't sure

of the answer or the question. Tom looked at Kelso and together they answered the question with a no.

The bottle of aspirin was pulled from her pocket as Jasmine showed the doctor. "Unless aspirin counts.", Jasmine interjected. "I gave him two. Kelso has not been attending to Campbell. It has been mostly me," she added.

The doctor now examined Kelso. He asked him to stand up and walk around. He tested his reflexes and examined his ears and eyes.

He told Nancy he probably should not be going with them but he was 99 percent sure he was no longer contagious—unless part of the equation was a virus. Dr. Evo told Nancy she could make the call.

The assessment was a matter of protocol. "As far as Tom and Jasmine was concerned, for the moment they were fine, but still would be allowed to go with them until they had been isolated for at least twenty-four hours. Then they should be examined and isolated again for another forty-eight hours. If there was so much as a pimple, a sniffle, a sneeze, a cough, or a wheeze ... Well, you get the picture. After the final examination, if there was absolutely nothing viral or bacterial present in or on their bodies, then they would be free to go. That was the contagion protocol as of twelve hours ago.", said Dr. Evo.

Nancy shook her head. "Negative. We can't wait. The FAA is closing down all non-major airstrips and will be using major hubs only to fly essential and military personnel. Also, I just got a text from Kemal, our pilot. He says the strip is being overrun with locals. People are trying to get into the private planes—successfully. He said not too many people know how to fly a small commercial jet. So far, he thinks he should be relatively safe for the time being. Let's get a move on. Safe or not, we all fly together, except for Campbell; he needs treatment now. We can all be under quarantine, and I will try to do my job remotely."

Penny smiled at Kelso, who did not smile back.

It was then that Nancy and the others heard Samuel scream. Jasmine, once again, pulled her gun and was through the door first. She squatted on the driveway, taking aim at the three individuals who were meandering down the driveway before anyone else had even looked through the window. She fired a warning shot above their heads. The two men and one woman made grunting, growling, and other inaudible sounds. The sound of the gunshot was enough of a warning for them to go in another direction. Jasmine would have preferred if they had turned around and headed back up the driveway. But instead, they just slightly turned to their left and walked toward a garden path that led to the backyard.

Tom joined her side with his gun drawn as well. "You go to the right of the path, and I'll take the left. If those few who went into the backyard are the only ones, we should be fine—that is if we leave right away. We just need to follow them so we know their position verses ours. Mechanically, they don't seem to be much of a threat. I don't know what we will be able to do to help them other than pray."

Jasmine, now up from the ground, grabbed his arm and pushed her chest next to his. "We won't be safe. I need to make the call. They are not going to take us. We are alone," Jasmine said.

Tom just pointed to the right.

Ten minutes passed.

Penny and Kelso were the last to make it onto the driveway, except for Campbell, who somehow had made it to the window and waited to see if they were going to leave him behind. Nancy was inside the car with Samuel, sitting in the back seat talking on the phone. She kissed Samuel on the forehead and stepped out of the car. "Everyone in the car, now. The suburbs of LA have been coded," she exclaimed. She refrained from saying the color and what it meant, but she knew things could get very ugly quickly.

Jasmine and Tom who had expanded their search down the street both made their way back onto the driveway.

"All clear," said Jasmine as she put her gun back behind her.

Tom made his way down the garden path to make sure he still saw the stragglers, which he did. Jasmine waited for Tom to let her know that the path was clear, but Tom just looked at her as he too put his gun back behind him. His military training was extensive, but Jasmine treated him like he was still in boot camp.

"We need to get Mr. Infectious into the back back seat with us. There's a military prop plane that will take him to the nearest base, until Dr. Evo, has found a place that will except him. As for Jasmine, Tom, and Kelso, you will come with me to Washington. And Samuel, Penny, Beverly, Jag, and Dr. Evo will wait it out at an isolated facility near the house for twenty-four hours and then another forty-eight hours until they have been cleared. We will meet up with them later," said Nancy, now addressing her sister. "Now in the car," she repeated.

Penny grabbed Kelso's hand. Penny, Kelso, Jasmine, and Tom wondered what had changed.

Tom and Jasmine went to get Campbell from inside the house. One of the stragglers was peering through the kitchen window. Campbell saw him and felt like he needed to let him in if he could. Campbell was also being called to wander as the clarity of his mind commenced to drain from his head. He remembered how he had sauntered aimlessly and stumbled to his feet and walked toward the kitchen. He remembered how he had felt free, nothing to do and nothing to think. He started to remember that there was someone else that was with him, but his thought was interrupted as he was quickly redirected by Tom and Jasmine. They both grabbed him by each of his arms. They were glad that he had already gotten up by himself, which had made their task a little easier.

There wasn't much room left when they finally got Campbell to the car. Dr. Evo knew now he was stuck with this bunch of strangers for a while longer. He tried not to think about his own family. He had one other thing on his mind. He took some extra syringes out of his black bag. "Nancy, give me five minutes," he said as he tapped on Tom's shoulder. He beckoned for him and Jasmine to come with him.

Nancy, who was in the driver's seat, shook her head profusely. Campbell, who was partially sitting on both their laps in the third-row seat, was pushed to the side with a grunt as both Tom and Jasmine hopped out of the car.

Dr. Evo, Jasmine, and Tom headed to the back of the house, where the three stragglers wandered. Jasmine and Tom held each person as Dr. Evo injected them in their shoulder with as much of the antibiotics as he could. Each person fell to his and her knees in pain. All three of them wished they could have done more as they headed back to the car.

"They will be all right?" asked Tom.

Dr. Evo turned and just looked at Tom and lifted his shoulders, but his conscience was at ease.

They arrived at the airstrip with little time to spare. The plane was already running. Kemal must have started the engines in anticipation of trouble. Beneath the plane was a small group of people, one with an assault rifle pointed at the plane. Two other people in the group were armed as well. There were several people standing in front of the plane.

Nancy and Jasmine consulted with each other as Tom listened in the background to their conversation. We need to get on the plane without being held hostage or overrun," said Nancy. "Any ideas?" She looked at Jasmine and behind her at Tom. "This is one of your areas of expertise?" Nancy put her arm around Jasmine.

Jasmine did not like being touched by Nancy but was glad to finally get the recognition.

There was nowhere to plan an ambush. They had to confront the situation straight on. Jasmine had come up with a couple of options, but it was Kelso who came up with the solution.

"Assuming Kemal knows what he's doing, have him back the plane up," said Kelso.

Nancy, along with everyone else, stood closed to the parked car about a thousand yards from the plane surveying the perimeter with binoculars. Nancy took out a small radio walkie-talkie and pushed the red button. Kemal immediately answered.

"We're behind you, 1,000 yards. There are no planes or people in this direction behind you. Can you taxi in this direction without being shot at? I don't think the man with the rifle would be so stupid, since he would be harming the very plane he is looking to hijack. I don't want to risk any of us getting shot at, especially my son. Otherwise, I would not ask you to do this," she said.

"It will be hard, but I will. I will use the thrust reverse as long as it's clear behind me, and I'll try not to set this plane on its tail," said Kemal.

The plane began to move—at first slowly, but then with great speed. "What is he doing? If he has to use the brakes, he'll put her on her butt," said Tom.

But the plane started to slow and eventually came to a stop about a hundred yards behind them.

The group of ten people came at them with shouts and guns pointed. A big burly fellow who stood about six foot three shouted, "You had better not be thinking of getting on our plane." It was the man with the long-range rifle, and he now stopped and started to situate himself to take aim.

The plane hatch opened, and a man in a military uniform came out. He introduced himself as Captain

Vick. He was well apprised of the situation, for as many people in the group who were holding guns in their hands found themselves tagged with a red laser mark on their chest or forehead. Captain Vick directed the hostiles as to what to do next. The man with the rifle immediately laid his gun in front of him and put his hands behind his head.

Jasmine stood in front of Samuel and Tom in front of Jasmine. Penny and Kelso stood behind Tom, but to his other side. Kelso was within inches of Tom's gun but realized there was no need for a gunfight. The skirmish had ended.

"Your plane should be here before we take off and has already been notified of local hostiles on the airstrips. From what the pilot told me, this is pretty friendly compared to other airstrips. There have been broadcasts of military casualties as well as civilian lives taken at other airfields. We best be on our way," said Captain Vick said as he looked toward the rest of the group that was not standing with Nancy.

"The plane that will take Campbell to the medical facility will also be taking us—Jasmine, Tom, Kelso, and me—to Washington DC. I'm sorry for the switch of plans, but think of yourself as sequestered," said Nancy, who had just become the enemy.

It was then that the small military plane landed behind them and several military men got out of the plane with guns of their own. Some of them were wearing medical masks. They pulled Campbell up and put his arms around their necks. They walked him onto the plane. Beverly and Jag, who had stayed in the car with Campbell and Silver, put Silver on his leash and followed Campbell toward the plane. They stopped when they met up with the rest of the group. Other than the plane ride, it was the last anyone would see of Campbell for a long while.

They watched as Campbell was escorted onto the plane. A couple of men stayed by the plane door.

"Should we refuse?" said Jasmine as she looked at Kelso, who was still had bluish-gray circles around his eyes on top of a seriously pale complexion.

Kelso let go of Penny's hand and walked forward and stood between Tom and Jasmine. He thought to speak but wanted to hear what Nancy had to say first. He hoped she had Penny's best interest at heart. Penny stepped forward and squeezed beside Kelso, once again grabbing her husband's hand.

Nancy positioned herself in front of Penny. "Penny, I am so sorry, but this is the way it has to be right now. It is just for a week or two at the most. If you want Kelso better, he needs to come with us."

Penny started to cry and raised Kelso's hand to her face. Kelso wanted to stay with Penny, but he had few options in his condition. All three of them were being strong-armed. He wondered if the extra military personnel was for his benefit.

Kelso took his hand back and held her face with both of his hands and smiled. "You want me well, right? You heard your sister; it will only be for a week or two. It will go by quickly for both of us." He'd never hated someone so much as he did Nancy at that moment. He kissed Penny on the forehead and turned around. He put his arm around Tom and walked toward the plane. Tom did a double take at Penny, who was hiding her face with her sleeve. Samuel came and grabbed his aunt's other hand.

Jasmine looked at Nancy. "I'm going to make your life hell," she said. She knew she was no longer on sabbatical. She followed Tom and Kelso onto the military plane. She lifted her phone to her ear.

Nancy ignored Jasmine. "I will save the formal introductions for when we're on the plane," she said Nancy. She turned around and beckoned everyone with a gesture of her sweeping arm to get aboard the plane; another door opened toward the front of the plane, and a small stairway dropped down.

Another man stepped off of the plane. "This is Colonel Jacobs, of the US Army. He will be accompanying some of us to the state's capitol," Nancy said. She leaned into the colonel's ear. "Who has the hostiles under siege?" she said, giving the captain a nudge.

"It was your pilot's idea. They had a few laser pointers in their supplies that they use for highlighting routes and locations on maps before they log in the coordinates." He smiled at Nancy. "They're still pointing them at their chests—except for the man with the rifle. It looks like they have one of the pointers targeted at his forehead."

Nancy turned and looked pathetically at the group of deviants—especially at the man with his hands behind his head and the assault rifle in front of him. It looked as if he might have peed.

Nancy and Colonel Jacobs were the last to board the military plane. Penny, Jag, Beverly, Dr. Evo, and Silver had already embarked on the commercial jet headed to Wyoming. Three more men stepped off the military plane. They waited for the planes to safely take off before confronting the small mob. The three men stayed behind and waited for another military convoy to come and then secured the airstrip.

Jasmine, Kelso, and Tom huddled under blankets in the corner of a military propellor plane. They were freezing cold. They could not believe how things had progressed. The plane was low on fuel, so they had minimal heat. They were told they would have to make at least two stops before reaching Washington. One would be to refuel. Kelso looked unusually sleepy despite the cold. Tom needed to keep everyone focused. He asked them all to say something that they were grateful for to make the time go by a little quicker.

Jasmine said that they were headed somewhere safe and that they had each other. Tom said the same but firmly patted Kelso's back to let him know he was included. The saving grace from his infection and having to be separated from Penny was the comforting thought that Penny and Samuel were with family. She most likely was the safest one out of all of them—at least much safer than they were right now.

Kelso's skin itched, but he tried not to scratch in front of the others. After they landed the first time to refuel, they were only two and half hours into their flight. The trip would take at least another three hours. Nancy told them to stay in the plane and to hunker down for the night. She would wake them when they approached Washington.

It didn't sound as if the location they landed at was secure. They had little food and practically no protection of their own. Nancy took the only guns the two possessed. Nancy handed them the cooler and groceries that Penny had packed. Penny had insisted that her sister take the food.

Jasmine made sandwiches and handed out miniature orange juices with bottled water. After they finished eating, Jasmine started to sing "I Surrender All" under her breath. Tom leaned in to hear what she was singing. He started to sing it as well but had to hum most of it since he didn't know the words.

Kelso at first did not agree that it was the appropriate time to sing songs, but as he listened, he was grateful for the sound of the hymn; it made him think of Christmas. He felt a little bit safer. He had envisioned himself inside their cozy house lounging back with Penny by a warm fire safe on the inside while carolers sang songs of praise and worship outside their front door. They would eventually get up and go to greet them. Although they never had carolers at their house, he imagined that was what it would have been like had they experienced such Christmas joy.

Kelso scratched his forearm. Flakes of skin fell to the ground, and other skin just peeled off. Jasmine held Kelso's hand as if to say, *It won't make it any better.*

"Kelso, do you know hymns?"

Kelso, embarrassed by his appearance and also his predicament, just shook his head. How the heck did his skin get so dry in such a short period of time? Then his head lifted. "I know a few. My favorite is 'Amazing

Grace.' I was a youth pastor before I met Penny." He looked for their reaction.

Tom continued to sing hymns under his breath. He was now singing "Amazing Grace." Kelso closed his eyes.

"We thought you might have been something like that at one time. Penny had said you once were very religious like Tom and me. Do you still believe?" asked Jasmine.

Kelso open his eyes and look into Jasmine's eyes. "I never stopped believing in Jesus. I just wasn't committed to Him. I wanted my own way, not growing my faith by reading the Bible to find out what God had to say to me. It was enough that I called myself a Christian and attended church. I thought I was going above and beyond what I was being called to by Him by being a youth pastor and dedicating my time. But lo and behold, He wanted my heart, not my resources and not my sense of propriety. Pride can be an awful thing." Kelso shook his head. "He wanted me to know Him personally and that, out of all the people, including myself, I was trying to impress, God, Himself, best loved me. He wanted me to trust in that love He had for me." Kelso who was surprised at his own confession. "I thought His ways were boring, but my life is much more exciting now that I am trusting Him with my life, very exciting in fact.

"But at the time, I became disillusioned. I felt like I had to be the answer and solve all the problems. There are just so many people who were bewildered and dejected that I just got very discouraged. The kids I worked with looked everywhere else for their purpose and solutions to their problems. They looked to themselves and others to fulfill their emptiness instead of God. They cried out to God by cutting themselves and experimenting with things that would keep them on the border of legally being high. Most of all, they did not want to be told what to do. If some of the young adults were to reluctantly submit to authority, their defiance would show itself in an aftermath of bad choices," said Kelso reflecting on his and their experiences.

Kelso looked at Jasmine, who was glued to his every word. Tom just stared at the floor. "I wasn't much different. I didn't want to be told what to do either, and I could relate in that way. They wanted a genuine leader. But I wasn't it; I was still worldly. But fortunately, there were always those teens who were more on target with their faith and pitched in to steer us back to God's grace and His provision. I was too young and full of myself to realize that I too had gone astray in my thoughts and actions. I knew, no matter how much I strayed, Jesus would always pick up the pieces because of His divine love for me. But I am certain I was grieving the holy spirit by the way I was living.

"When Penny and I met, I was void of all Christian activities. I thought that, at some point, I would convert her over to Christianity after we were married. And then it dawned on me that I wasn't sure anymore what I believed. I did 't feel anything anymore, yet I always knew there was more. Eventually I came across Christians like yourself who were praying for me. I started to be drawn back into fellowship by the truths I had once believed. I started to attend a men's Bible study on Wednesday night, which drew me further into the Bible. I realized I had become a little disillusioned. I was looking at others in the church instead of directly committing myself to Jesus. It was as if I expected other people to carry me by their faith in God.

"Now that this has happened to me and others, I believe even more strongly that there is a purpose in all this. I've been praying for those children in that youth program ever since I realized I needed to repent and ask for forgiveness for walking away. I pray those children are no longer bewildered or dejected and that they know their genuine leader, our shepherd, Jesus Christ. I know that some of those kids who never lost their focus are still praying for me today. I have committed my life to Him whether He heals me or not," Kelso concluded without any hesitation.

Jasmine was crying. Tom didn't look up.

"I came to accept Christ as Messiah, the Son of God, who died for my sins, after my tour in Iraq. I had the same feeling you had; there had to be more to all of this, but that truth led me in the other direction. Instead of doubting His insufficiency, I saw the darkness of humanity and knew there had to be a God who accounted for both the good and the evil—that there had to be a divine purpose in both, that without a God who is 100 percent holy, there cannot be the dichotomy of good and evil. If there wasn't light to break through the darkness, then there would be no light at all. Does that make sense?" Tom stopped and looked at both Jasmine and Kelso.

Jasmine nodded, while Kelso told him he would have to think on it for a while—that he was with him up until the light and dark.

Jasmine smiled, and Tom continued. "What I saw

in Iraq there among the soldiers and civilians is nothing compared to what we have in the United States. The poverty level and lack of freedoms were the most serious factors. I have reported some of it to officials and different charitable organizations, but modest improvements could be made. My heart broke into a thousand pieces. People had no place to confess any of their sins because it was all being accepted. No one could heal because no one would let them be sick. Everything was fair in war and war or however that old cliché goes. I continued to try to do what I could. Finally, things started to change. Anyway, I came home in a fog to my wife, Jasmine. She was a new Christian at that time. And the rest is history."

Jasmine looked into his eyes and smiled.

It was at that moment the ground beneath them shook. They heard in the distance people shouting. There was a wave of warmth that came over them. "It's not nuclear but it's definitely a bomb; the explosion had a small radius," said Jasmine.

Jasmine's heart was racing. She now addressed Tom. "I made the call on the way into the plane. I am supposed to help with the Arab crisis, which I agreed to since I would have been forced into it anyway by your government." She hated being back in the thick of things. She was wondering if she would be able to handle it.

Kelso looked at Tom. Tom wasn't sure what to say now the cat was out of the bag. He knew that they would be OK but not because of either Nancy's or Jasmine's ties with their governments.

"I sure as heck would like to know what kind of bomb that was?" he asked.

Jasmine continued, ignoring Tom's question for now. "I received the intel that I wanted as well. The contagion is everywhere, Israel too. Anyway, when we get to Washington, my people will be waiting for us to take me to the Israeli embassy. They will give all of us safe transportation and an isolated place for us to stay within the embassy until we're cleared. They have doctors as well to care for Kelso, but that's where our fight will begin. Kelso tested positive at the hospital, but he's a step ahead of everyone else who has been infected. His progression has not only slowed, but the dry skin is actually a good sign of recovery. No one is getting better, only worse. At least that's what our doctors are saying," she whispered.

"I'm not sure that the Israeli government will be able to keep us with you as visitors," said Kelso.

"If we move quickly enough, our chances are best," she replied. "They've been tracking us since I made the call. Since that was an exothermic explosion with dark clouds, we can assume it was a liquid combustible bomb. My people know where we are and how to extract us from here if necessary—in case there are any other explosions. It won't be easy, since I'm on foreign soil. As far as Kelso is concerned, my people can get the US president's consent afterward and before Nancy can think to get an injunction for you, Kelso."

Nancy came back on board the plane, with a few new faces and military personnel. As soon as she entered the plane, the door shut, and the plane started to taxi down the runway. She looked over at Kelso and smiled. He did not smile back. The plane now seemed warmer.

Jasmine retrieved more blankets and some pillows.

She put several blankets on top of Kelso and gave him a pillow. She then sat down on the other side of Kelso. Tom and Jasmine sat with Kelso between them and talked to each other in hushed voices.

# Chapter 12

## The Escape

*J*asmine plugged her satellite attachment into the audio port of her iPhone. It gave her a secure frequency for transmissions, as well as registered the latitude and longitude coordinates of the plane. She showed Tom. They both stood, made their way to one of the windows, and looked out.

It would be ten minutes before they landed. If Nancy knew anyone was coming for them, they would not be allowed off of the airplane. Or they would have a strong military presence to assist with their transfer. She looked at Tom. He watched her eyes for suggestions. Jasmine looked over at Kelso.

Kelso was sitting up and instinctively laid his bag beside him. Jasmine started stretching as one of Nancy's escorts watched. Tom went and blocked the view of his wife from the armed military personnel and started to stretch as well. Kelso, who was a little off balance, yawned as he stood up and bent down to touch his toes. "Long flight,", Kelso said as he looked at Jasmine, who was now in a scripted yoga pose, and rolled his eyes.

Another man, also armed, approached the back of the plane. "I'm glad to see you're all up and moving around," he said. "Officer Preston and I will be escorting you to a secure location for the night. Nancy will meet up with you sometime tomorrow when you've had a good night's sleep. Gather your belongings; we should be landing shortly."

"Please," Jasmine said. "Requests go better with please and thank you. Would you not agree?" She paused for him to introduce himself.

"Captain David S. Bond. And like James, I prefer things stirred and not shaken. So you would do well not to piss me off, Jasmine," said Captain Bond.

Tom, stepped forward to let him know that he could take him, gun or no gun. Jasmine made a facial expression of indifference and continued stretching, putting one of her arms behind her head and pulling on it with her other arm.

The plane landed with no Israeli intelligence in sight. Jasmine had expected as much, but Kelso kept looking around. Tom tried to take Kelso's mind off what was about to happen. He put his arm around Kelso's shoulder and made idle chat about how he could go for a thick juicy steak, a side salad, and a loaded potato if they were allowed to order in. Kelso looked at Tom like he was crazy but then saw the black limousine pull up beside a parked Ford Escort and police car.

Nancy and some others from her party who were also on the plane were already in a Lincoln MKZ turning onto a small side road. The captain waited for the officials to make their way to him, which they did quickly, holding FBI badges in their hands.

"Sorry, Captain Bond, we need to steal these folks

from you. We have authorization to take possession of Kelso, Jasmine, and Tom," said Agent Garrett.

The captain looked at their badges and then at the diplomatic flags attached to the black limousine.

"It's part of a diplomatic recognizant initiative with Israel," said Agent Garrett. He handed him a piece of paper with a raised seal.

The captain knew this was over his pay grade and looked behind him to Officer Preston, motioning to him to make a call by making a phone with his hand and putting it up to his ear. Jasmine knew they were in trouble. The two policemen approached. The driver of the Ford Escort stayed in the car.

Jasmine, Tom, and Kelso made their way to the limousine, knowing that the custody battle had just began. The captain told them not to move until they had this squared away, but Jasmine just looked at him and smiled over her shoulder as they walked over to a man who was holding the limousine door open for them. Kelso, Tom, and Jasmine slid into the tan leather seats. Jasmine tapped on the window separating them from the driver.

The driver and another Israeli agent, who Jasmine had worked with and knew well, smiled at her and handed her a small flash drive.

"An expensive price to pay for your assistance," the man said in Hebrew.

Jasmine smiled as she took the hard drive and put it into a secure pocket sewn into the side of her brassiere. She told the driver to go quickly and not stop, also speaking in Hebrew.

Just as they turned onto the side road and started to speed up, a Lincoln MKZ passed them.

"Are we going to be OK?" asked Tom. He looked at Jasmine.

"I'm pretty sure we should be able to make this work for a short while, but we should come up with a plan C," she replied.

Kelso, who had his head resting against the back seat, looked up at the both of them and smiled. He put his head back and closed his eyes.

Penny, Samuel, and the others arrived at Nancy's country house later than expected. They'd had to take several detours to avoid traffic. It was past time for dinner, but Penny was sure her mom and dad would have made something for them to eat.

As the car pulled up, Penny's mom and dad stood on the front porch and waved. There was a man standing beside them in camouflage. She realized they would not be able to make contact until, once again, they were totally cleared.

They were quarantined to a makeshift habitation of tents, with heaters; televisions; and homemade appetizers of small sandwiches, chicken fingers, cheese sticks, and a cheese and vegetable tray for those who were more health conscience. The snacks had her mother's signature— beautifully arranged and not overdone. Penny once again felt sick but ate some of the crackers next to the cheese plate anyway.

Their mom and dad had been hard at work trying

to come up with comfortable accommodations for them. They knew it was only temporary until they were completely cleared of the contagion.

The perimeter was now being secured by armed guards. Where all the extra people were going to stay was a mystery. The reported fatality toll was now in the hundreds of thousands spanning across the globe. It was spreading quickly, and the virus strain was mutating, which caused hemorrhaging of the eyes and failure of the liver in certain parts of the country.

Penny had time to think on the plane about everything. Her nausea came back again, which contributed to her eating lightly. Dr. Evo was suspicious of her condition and wanted to run one more test on her when they got into their quarters.

Dr. Evo was especially fond of Penny. He sat next to her, arm touching arm on a make-shift couch in their tent. He looked at her and smiled. She smiled back at him. too tired to move away.

He handed her a stick. "You do know what to do?" he.

Penny's eyes sparkled. "Yes, but I am not. Really?" she asked.

She realized it was a real possibility. She and Kelso did not consider themselves trying to have kids, but there were those times of unprotected sex. "I can't wait. I hope you're right, Doc."

Penny headed out of the tent and into the trees. *Two minutes,* she thought to herself.

# Chapter 13

## *The Reunion*

The plane landed. Armed guards surrounded the plane. The door to the plane opened and extended a stairway. Kelso slowly escorted himself off of the plane. Penny quickly wobbled to Kelso. It had been three months. She had been by herself except for the two little ones hidden within her.

Kelso hugged her, although he was not able to expend much energy. She looked up at his face, which was pale and gaunt. "You don't look so well. But I guess you know that. So what's next?" she asked. She, on the other hand, was healthy and was rounder in size than when they'd last been together.

Kelso grinned. "We have options, lots of options. There are places that are viable, but of course they have their pros and cons. Where would you like to go?" he asked as they walked toward the airport.

Penny was glad to hold his hand again. "Where is the least likely place that I will get sick and we can live modestly but protected?" she asked. She wasn't sure whether or not that was a dumb question. She knew that Kelso was no longer contagious, but the illness had taken its toll. He gave her another squeeze with the arm that he had around her.

"I have a lot to tell you," she said quietly.

"I have a lot to tell you as well. Jasmine and Tom are fine. They never got sick, thank the Lord, and they were around me quite a bit."

Penny made a face. "They were rubbing off on you."

He smiled again at her as he reached for the door and let Penny slide past him.

Kelso was about as happy as he could remember within the last couple of months. Times had been better, but he hadn't had the same appreciation for the things he now did. "Penny, you know that Jasmine has a lot more in common with you than you know," he said.

Penny squeezed his hand. "How so?"

"For one thing, she is also Jewish as well as African American," he replied.

Penny looked at Kelso. Her eyes told him he was wrong, but she was willing to listen. "She said she was Jewish? How could I have not known that?"

Kelso grinned. "You don't know how Jewish. She works for the Israeli government."

The airport became busy with activity, guards and police running through the airport.

A National Reconnaissance agent stopped them in the airport and turned Kelso's tag around on his neck. He immediately pulled out his own badge. Agent Rastas was of Jamaican descent but born and raised in the United States. "Keep this handy, man, and do not let anyone take it from you." The man looked him up and down. "How did you get this? Is your wife accounted for? I don't see her badge." He continued to look Kelso and Penny over. "Hell, you look like an infected. Your wife, who is she?"

Kelso looked at him. "Does she have to be anyone? She's with me."

The tall man in the suit continued. "I'm not sure how you were able to get this far. If you didn't have this badge with the presidential seal, you would be waiting for clearance with everyone else."

Kelso looked around and realized there was no unauthorized civilians or persons anywhere. "I take it back, Penny. We may be limited in our travels," he said.

The agent grabbed the badge again and read it closely. "Do you need an escort, Kelso? To where will you be traveling? Most cities and airports have been shut down, but you know that," he stated.

Kelso wasn't sure now about the logistics of their situation and didn't want to seem like a lamb in a lion's den, but he had only questions. He'd thought they would be able to get onto another plane and fly somewhere safer. Jasmine and Tom would make this so easy. "I suppose we could use an escort," he said. "So what is this badge good for?"

He anticipated the agent's next question. Standing six four, he looked down on them, literally. He had started to take pity on them. Normally, he did not give two cents about people, except those closest to him. But with everything that was happening, he was obliged to help the couple out, one infected but apparently cleared and the other naive and perhaps pregnant. "I can take you to a base. That badge around your neck can do a lot for you but not if you are on your own in with the masses." His Jamaican accent was strong.

Kelso glanced at Penny and held her hand a little firmer. "What are our choices?" he asked.

"There's an old military base in Aberdeen, Maryland, in Harford County," said the officer. It's being reinstated for special personnel. It's old, built in 1917, but still functional. You'll have to make yourself useful. Money will only take you so far these days."

Penny thought she had heard about that base but couldn't remember what she'd heard. "Wasn't there an incident about twenty years ago regarding some women?" she asked. "What are the other choices?"

The agent looked at Penny as if what was in the past was not important, but Penny considered everything— the past, present, and future—in all her decisions. History had always been important to her and Kelso. Whether it was superstition or the prevailing facts, she believed the history and/or just the "vibe" of a place could tell a person whether there was safety.

"The other choices around here are Anacostia-Bolling, Andrews, Langley, Fort Myers, Fort Mead, and the list goes on. You would have to risk getting on another military plane to get to the ones down the coast. The escort would still have to stand, for me to call it in," the agent informed them.

"Can we go to Langley? That is where Nancy is. Wouldn't we need a high-level clearance? Or is there a place we could stay outside of the facility where we'd be safe? I always wanted to live in Virginia. Nancy wrote me this morning that, if I had to do what I had to do, she would accept it, but she would be at Langley, and there would be a place for us. I did purposely leave everything electronic behind so she couldn't track me since you said I shouldn't let her know I was meeting you here. You know she's like that." She paused and looked up at Kelso and wondered if she was rambling. "Anyway, I won't say too much more except that was a little trick I picked up with Jasmine. She is so clever not to leave an electronic signature that anyone would be able to pick up on."

Nancy was the last person Kelso ever wanted to see again. He didn't want to fall into another trap. It was because of her he almost became a human sacrifice. Kelso needed to make a decision, but he wasn't sure where else to go.

He knew the battle would start all over again as soon as he saw Nancy, but this time it would be for Penny. She would do anything to keep her little sister safe; she had taken God out of the equation from the beginning— not recognizing that another force had been at work. It was God who'd kept him safe, and it was God who would protect Penny. He felt like Langley was the wrong decision. But anywhere they went, he knew they would be discovered.

The agent became very agitated. "Who is it you're trying to lose that can get you into Langley?" asked Agent Rastas. "We had better start walking." He put his hand on Kelso's shoulder.

Kelso wondered whether their conversation had just put them in jeopardy and whether Agent Rastas could be trusted. Kelso once again said a silent prayer.

Agent Rastas looked across at Kelso and put his arm around his shoulders and leaned in close. "You know, man, we have a saying back in Jamaica. 'Better a dry crust eaten in peace than a house filled with feasting—and conflict.'" He paused. "Except in Jamaica we say it a little different. It's a house full of love, but I think it means the same."

Kelso exchanged a smile with the agent. "Proverbs 17:1, if I remember correctly," he said. "Where do you think we should go?"

"The facility in Aberdeen, Maryland. My family and I are there. So far, we have been disease free, thank God above. I'm not sure about the bad situation that occurred twenty years ago, but once you get there you can see for yourself what you think."

Agent Rastas, Kelso, and Penny arrived at the gate. A man with a mask wearing camouflage approached the black sedan, while two other military persons with masks guarded the gate. From above the gate Kelso could see two of what looked like recently constructed towers with military short- and long-range equipment attached to every side of the towers. He wasn't sure if he would feel safe or entrapped.

Agent Rastas pushed the button to lower the car window, granting access and greeted the man at his car window. Agent Rastas read his name tag, Sergeant Mark Riddle.

"You need to back up and go down this road." The sergeant pointed to the road in front of him. "Make the first right and there's a place for you to park and wait until someone can inspect you and your vehicle."

Agent Rastas put the car in reverse. "He looked behind him and nodded. It was as if he was letting them know it was OK. He pulled onto the side road. Eventually, they reached the right turn they'd been directed to by the sergeant. As the car started to turn right, something didn't feel right. They were turning into a crowded parking lot.

"Oh no. This cannot be good," Kelso said and looked to his wife, whose eyes were as wide as walnuts.

Agent Rastas looked at him and shook his head as if he was waiting for his signal. "OK, boss, I'm taking you somewhere else."

Before anyone had anytime to object, he put his vehicle into reverse one more time, and the vehicle was on the road. "We can wait it out until there's no one else in line. I'll call it in and let them know what your credentials are. I'll find out if there's another place we can temporarily go." Agent Rastas pushed a button on his steering wheel and told his car to dial White House Operations.

"Pizza Hut," said Adam.

"Hi. This is Agent Rastas and we have essential persons who cannot be exposed, level 5 with seal but no clearances. We need Aberdeen."

"No clearances, you say." said Adam. "This is one for the books. His first name isn't Kelso, is it?"

"Yes, it is. How did you know?" asked Agent Rastas.

"We need to switch to a secure line. But it's safe to say that you and your party should be prepared to be extracted shortly. From where you are, there's a secured facility about a mile from you. I'm sending your coordinates to your GPS device in your car. Do not go with anyone who doesn't have the proper credentials," Adam warned. "You should not let your party out of your sight for reasons of their safety. Go live if necessary."

A blimp appeared on the GPS screen. "Thanks, I'll call you if there are any obstacles," said Agent Rastas.

"Gee, Agent Rastas, count me in too," said Kelso.

Agent Rastas turned around and looked at Kelso.

"Count me in as an obstacle. Can you let me in on what the plan is now before we go anywhere else?" asked Kelso.

Other cars started to follow Agent Rastas's maneuver and pull out. "I will as we drive. We cannot be followed, and many people are in the same situation as we are. They don't want to risk being exposed and yet are deemed essential, but they don't have your credentials. We have to move it if I have a chance of these bobos not following us. So with your permission …" As Agent Rastas said this, he already had his sedan out of park and was speeding down the two-lane road.

Kelso grabbed Penny's hand.

"Never a dull moment. Maybe we should say a prayer," Penny said and smiled at Kelso.

"Not a bad idea," chimed in Agent Rastas. "Lord Jesus, please protect us in this situation and get us to where we need to be."

Kelso was a little peeved that Rastas had chimed in on their prayer, but they both said amen. Penny looked up and smiled again at Kelso and squeezed his hand.

"I understand a little more about the Lord now. I don't believe that Jesus is just our Messiah. I believe He is the world's Messiah and that He is the Christ, God's Son. I don't understand everything, but Dr. Evo explained a lot."

"Is that your good news you were saving for me?" asked Kelso.

"That is the best news. The good news is that we are having twins. I can't stop thanking the Lord. It was so hard not to tell you. I needed to see you in person so you would not worry or talk me out of coming to be with you."

Agent Rastas moved his rearview mirror and glanced at Kelso's face. Kelso saw that Agent Rastas was teary-eyed. "You are good people. You will do the right thing." The car slowed and made a right turn and then a left into a parking lot. "We are here," he said. He drew his gun. "I am here to protect you. We need to get you into this building. An extract team is on its way."

Several civilian cars had followed them, and other people were coming from different directions. Some looked infected, as they were disheveled and could not keep their balance.

The building didn't look like a secure facility as Adam had said it would be. Agent Rastas got out of his car and wondered where the calvary was. Just as Rastas was about to fire his gun into the air, about a dozen soldiers filed out of the main building doors. "On the ground," they shouted to those approaching the car. "Agent Rastas?" asked the corporal.

Agent Rastas showed him his badge. The corporal nodded as the soldiers blocked the car from the intruders so that Penny and Kelso could get out of the car and follow the corporal and some of his men into the building.

Kelso sensed that something wasn't right. He looked back and saw the enlarging crowd and Agent Rastas trying to get back into his car. A canister of tear gas was used on the crowd that was immediately behind the black sedan. *Oh, no you don't*, Kelso said to himself and took off running toward the car.

Agent Rastas looked up and saw Kelso running toward him. He quickly started to run toward the building. "I'm not essential enough to be extracted," he said as he met Kelso midway. They both continued to run toward the building; officers from around the building rushed forward to police the crowd.

"But you were assigned to us, so you should automatically have that clearance. Heck, I don't have that clearance. But I know one thing, if you don't go, I won't go. Plus I don't know that we can trust these guys," said Kelso.

The large area expanded for as far as they could see; the mountains started to shrink as more and more vehicles flowed into the parking lot. The vehicles were directed to one area or another. Agent Rastas was immediate thankful and loyal to Kelso and Penny as he thought about his own family and their options. Once inside the compound, he and his family would be more likely to excepted now he was with Kelso and Penny.

The door automatically opened as they approached. It was as if they were surrendering their souls. They were right in that Agent Rastas and his family would be accepted due to his fast acquaintance with Kelso and Penny.

This was the safe haven for Kelso and Penny. She would have access to everything she needed for a safe birth for their twins. Unfortunately, it was a tradeoff.

Although Kelso, by the help of God, was healing, his health would still be weakened by the deal he made. He would become the unwilling guinea pig, enduring many tests, trials, and experiments that would impede his recovery. Kelso was a ground zero patient, but he was one of the few who was improving.

They were surrounded and welcomed by Penny's family, who she thought she had left in Wyoming. It made her extremely uneasy. It was only Dr. Evo's shake of his head that let her know he'd had no idea that everyone had been compromised and she needed to stay calm.

Safe abodes were now mostly limited to government structures. Penny tried not to be angry. It was for the sake of their twins who rested inside of her. But for Kelso, she was livid. She consoled herself by thinking of how eventually things could turn around if they found a cure.

The agreement between the government and their family was in place until something better would be negotiated. Kelso voluntarily agreed to three months of experimentation with no blood transfusions but with the giving of blood, among other tests. It was in exchange for the ability to indefinitely stay in a place that was deemed safe for him and his family. He would also continue to get treatment.

Jasmine and Tom proceeded to assist the Israeli government in different matters with the same agreement but with a more limited time frame. They safely lived in the hills of Israel, which was not affected by the contagion like other parts of the world. They both remained in constant contact with Kelso and/or Penny.

A peace came over both Penny and Kelso. They did the right thing, even if it didn't seem like it was the easiest thing. They held hands as they were escorted to their family's new living quarters.

Printed in the United States
by Baker & Taylor Publisher Services